The Charm Bracelet

The Charm Bracelet

SUSAN PAGE DAVIS

CHAPTER ONE

Portland, Maine

Lisa felt a definite lowering of her expectations as she walked briskly from the jewelry store into the mall, the myriad golden tokens on her charm bracelet clinking delicately.

The man she had planned to spend the rest of her life with walked beside her, a satisfied smile lingering on his face.

Time to face facts, Lisa told herself. Their goals diverged. Their secret longings were poles apart. She ought to have seen it sooner.

"Lunch in the Terrace Room?" Bryan asked.

"All right." She didn't really feel like lunch, but it was Valentine's Day, and this date was supposed to be special.

He put one hand lightly on the back of her hunter green wool coat, steering her toward the escalator at the center of the mall. It led to the upper level shops and the Terrace Room, a cut above the eateries in the ground level food court.

She had dated Bryan for more than three years. Before the first year was over, she had decided that she loved him. She had seen him exclusively since then, twice a month, when he came home from Portland to visit his parents. Three months ago she had taken a new job in the city and found a reasonably-priced apartment. She was closer to Bryan, and they went out every weekend now, and at last she felt she was getting to know him. But what she had learned was a disappointment.

It was Saturday, and they had both kept Valentine's Day free, but Bryan had called her that morning full of apologies. He claimed there was no way out of working the evening shift, and transformed their special dinner date to lunch at the mall.

They paused at the bottom of the escalator, waiting for the right moment to step on. As she reached for the railing, the charms swayed, glittering.

For her birthday the first year they dated, Bryan had bought her the gold bracelet. She had been overwhelmed with joy. Too expensive. So beautiful.

You deserve it, he'd said.

Dangling from it was a perfect little golden dog. A German shepherd. Bryan had a German shepherd.

Lisa was not a dog person.

On every special occasion for the last three years, Bryan had bought her another charm to add to the bracelet. Some were truly lovely. Others were whimsical. Lisa loved the bracelet. At least, she had for a long time.

She raised her foot and stepped onto the moving step of the escalator with Bryan.

Somehow, she misjudged. Her mind had been elsewhere. She plunged forward and found herself sprawling on the escalator.

"Lisa! Are you all right?"

His hand was firm under her elbow as he tried to help her rise.

Lisa attempted to stand, but her wrist was held captive.

"Oh, no. My bracelet is caught."

"Lisa!"

People on the down side of the escalator stared at them.

"Stop this thing!" Bryan yelled, staring toward the approaching landing above them. They were nearly halfway up. "Somebody shut this thing off!"

Lisa tugged at the bracelet, but it wouldn't budge. She dropped her purse and brought her left hand over to try to disentangle it.

"I can't get it loose," she gasped.

"Break it!"

She pulled hard. Nothing happened.

"There's an emergency switch at the top, isn't there?" She tried to keep the fear from her voice.

Bryan ran up the steps, pushing past a woman laden with packages. Lisa stooped, jerking at the bracelet. *If I pull too hard and it breaks, I'll fall down the stairs!*

The woman above her stepped off onto the second floor. The step just ahead of Lisa flattened out magically. She stared in fascination, wondering what would happen when her hand reached the edge of the grid, where the stairs disappeared under the floor.

She pulled again, hard. The gold chain tightened around her wrist.

Then everything stopped moving.

"Lisa!" Bryan was beside her again. "Sweetheart, are you hurt?"

"I don't think so. Not yet. It's tight, though. Whatever you did, thank you!"

"Can you unhook it?"

"No, the clasp seems to be stuck in there."

"We've got to get somebody to help you." He looked around frantically. "Get security!" he yelled at a group of staring shoppers.

Three security guards and the mall manager arrived panting. Bryan was pushed out of the way as they crowded around Lisa, each thinking he could solve the problem in an instant.

She sat for five humiliating minutes, trying to hold back the tears, as they pulled, twisted, swore, apologized, tugged, and fiddled. The chain was biting into her wrist, not sharply, but her hand began to turn red. Finally one of the guards called for a rescue unit, and another went down the idle escalator to divert the shoppers who kept stopping at the base, looking up blankly, wondering why the stairs were not moving, and what was wrong with the blonde who sat on the top step, her coat half on and half off, her face scarlet.

Twelve minutes passed before the EMTs arrived. Lisa was too warm with her winter coat on. She shrugged her left arm out of its sleeve, but the right was doomed to wear the coat.

She had plenty of time to think about her relationship with Bryan, as her fingers went numb and slowly turned purple.

Since the German shepherd, he had bought her more charms that, to him at least, signified the progress of their life together. A mortar board for Lisa's graduation from college. A dollar sign when she'd landed her first "real" job, at a small advertising agency near home. A tiny stethoscope; Bryan was an intern. A snowflake the first Christmas. A tiny Cupid at Valentine's. A sailboat, for the outing they'd had on her next birthday.

It was about the time the sailboat charm was added that Lisa began to wonder when he would propose. The charm bracelet was lovely, full of precious memories, but her ring finger was conspicuously bare.

He loved her. He said so. He even talked in general terms about their future together. But he never came right down to it, somehow. And he always had to be back in Portland early Sunday, so he could never stay and accompany her to church. Lisa pushed aside her misgivings.

The next Christmas he had bought her a minuscule snowman; Valentine's Day an 18-karat gold I-heart-U. A tennis racquet, when Bryan won the hospital's annual tournament. It went on.

This winter she had moved to Portland, taking a more lucrative position at a bigger agency. Bryan had bought a gold artist's palette charm for Christmas, celebrating her position as art director at Clark Media. But Lisa didn't paint. She drew. Her commercial art was done mostly in pen and ink.

Now that they were seeing each other more often, she had really thought—

But why? she asked herself bitterly, as they waited for the EMTs. *Three years of my life. Do I really want to keep waiting?*

The mall manager was nervous. He had finally stopped apologizing, but hovered fretfully at the top of the stairs, twisting his ring and muttering.

Bryan sat beside her, speaking soothingly, but checking his watch every few seconds.

Two men in uniform arrived at the bottom of the stairs, escorted by one of the mall security guards. They came up quickly, carrying their medical bags.

"What seems to be the trouble?" the first one asked. His smile was the brightest thing Lisa had seen all day. She wondered if he would have smiled if her blood had been spattered about.

Bryan stood and moved aside, standing with one hand on the rail.

Lisa nodded toward her numb right hand. "I tripped on the stairs, and my bracelet got caught in the machinery. We've tried everything, but I can't get loose."

"Let's take a look."

The EMT knelt on the steps, bending low over her hand. His dark hair was casually fluffy, as though he had just blow-dried it. *Why can't Bryan's hair look like that, instead of meticulously combed?*

Annoyed with herself, Lisa looked up into the eyes of the EMT's partner, who stood a couple of steps below. He was short, about five-foot-six, stocky, and so young she thought he must have just passed his exam for the job.

His smile was endearing. "I'm Jimmy. He's Steve. He's really good. Get you out of here in no time."

"Thanks." Lisa couldn't help smiling back.

Steve was repeating all the motions the security guards had tried.

"Amazing that didn't break," he muttered.

Lisa realized her chin was almost touching the shoulder of his blue uniform jacket, and she raised her head a little, leaning back away from him. He was tall and lean, the opposite of Jimmy, and his intent brown eyes gave her a strange feeling. She looked away.

"Hmm. We may have to cut this thing off you."

"Uh, well—" Lisa shot a glance up at Bryan.

"It's 18-karat gold, buddy." Bryan clipped out the words.

"I think I can cut through one link and get the lady free," Steve said, "but part of the bracelet is really meshed in there. I'm not sure we can salvage the whole thing."

"Do what you have to," Lisa said, not looking at Bryan.

"All right. Jimmy, we got some wire cutters somewhere?"

"Sure, in the truck. I'll get them." The young man skipped down the steps and trotted toward the mall entrance.

There was a shrill beep from above them, and Bryan pulled his pager from his jacket pocket.

"Lisa, I've got to call the hospital. Will you be all right for a couple of minutes?"

"Of course. By the time you get back, I'll be free."

Bryan nodded and stepped away, along the mezzanine, taking out his cell phone. The manager watched him forlornly.

"So, you're a woman of many charms," Steve quipped.

She smiled faintly. It wasn't the first time she'd heard the remark, and it was starting to irritate her.

"You're not in pain, are you?"

"No, but my hand is asleep. Bryan looked at it. He thinks I'll be okay, as long as you can get me out of here quickly."

"Your husband's an expert?"

"Yes, he's an expert. He's a doctor. But he's not my husband." It came out more tartly than she had intended.

"Sorry." Steve glanced down the stairway, but Jimmy was not yet in sight. A guard was tying a cord across the bottom of the escalator, and a girl stood near him holding a hand-lettered sign that read *Out of Order*.

"Am I right that he bought this for you?"

"Yes, and all fifteen charms."

"So, how much do you love this bracelet?"

"I'm starting to hate it," she admitted.

"Ooh, there's more to that story."

She shrugged. "Am I going to have to pay to have the escalator fixed?"

"Ha! That manager looked positively green. Probably figures you're going to sue."

"I'm not the litigating kind." Lisa leaned back and tried not to look at him. It was just that he was so…unlike Bryan.

She was angry with herself for thinking he was good looking, then even madder because it made her feel guilty. Bryan was her boyfriend. A little voice in her brain argued that, other than the weighty charm bracelet and their mutually accepted arrangement of exclusive dating, Bryan had no claim on her.

Their relationship seemed to have stagnated, somewhere between the sailboat and the tennis racquet. In the three months she had lived in town, he had been to church with her once. If he wasn't working, there was always an excuse, and she realized it was becoming a sticking point for her. If he didn't want to worship, was his heart what she had imagined it to be?

"There's Jimmy." Steve nodded toward the busy floor far below. She picked out the young EMT in the crowd. They waited in silence as he circumvented the flimsy new barrier and mounted the stairs with a small toolbox.

Steve took it from him and opened it on the top step.

"Okay, hold still now. I'm going to cut through one link. If you take the bracelet to the jeweler where Dr. Charming bought it, they should be able to fix it for you."

"Cute," she said grimly.

She looked up at the ceiling as he took her wrist in one hand and slid one blade of the cutters between her skin and the gold chain. His fingers were warm, and his touch was delicate. She could tell his hands were bigger than Bryan's without looking.

Suddenly her hand pulled free, and she rubbed the deep crease the bracelet had left and stared at Steve.

He bent over the little pile of links and charms, his eyes inches from the crack that had swallowed part of the golden strand.

"One of your charms seems to be mangled in there." He made another clip with the wire cutters, and held up the bracelet. "Which of your baubles is missing?"

She took it and held it up, racking her memory, counting over the love tokens one by one.

"The new one. He bought it for me today, right before this happened."

"What is it?"

"Does it matter?" She couldn't help remembering how Bryan had lingered over a tiny golden sports car, then reluctantly let the clerk steer them toward symbols more appropriate for Valentine's Day.

"Not really. Just curious." He was working at the crack with a thin tool.

"It's a gold filigree heart." She gasped as the blood flowing into her right hand made it prickle.

"You okay?"

"Pins and needles."

"Jimmy, check this lady's wrist while I see if I can retrieve her heart."

Lisa smiled wryly.

Jimmy took her hand gingerly, something like awe on his face.

"Can you feel that, miss?"

"Yes. I'll be fine, I'm sure."

"Well, looks like your heart is beyond repair." Steve extracted a barely recognizable wad of smashed gold wire.

"Tell me about it." Lisa held out her hand and looked at the debris.

"Take it back to the jewelry store."

"You think they can repair it?"

Steve shrugged. "Maybe the mall management will pay to replace it."

Lisa wasn't sure she wanted to replace it. Her wrist was so much lighter without the bracelet, and somehow her spirits were lighter, too. She looked up, realizing the two men were watching her closely.

"Thank you very much, gentlemen."

"You're welcome." Steve extended a hand and she took it, rising slowly.

"So, I didn't ruin the escalator?"

Steve smiled. "It should be fine. Jimmy, go down and tell the guard to start it up and see if everything's okay."

He picked up the toolbox and moved Lisa onto the carpeted floor of the second story.

She slipped her right arm out of her coat sleeve.

"Here comes your fiancé." Steve nodded toward his right, and Lisa turned to follow his gaze. Bryan and the manager were walking swiftly toward them.

"He's not my fiancé."

"All right, boyfriend."

She said nothing.

"He can't be your brother. A brother might buy a girl a dog charm, but not a Cupid."

Lisa felt hostility rising toward him. "Look, you're not so charming yourself. I appreciate your help, but my love life is none of your business."

He held out his hands in protest. "You're right. Sorry. That was unprofessional. I don't usually do that sort of thing." He looked at her keenly, as though he wanted to say more.

Lisa felt her face reddening under his scrutiny. "And I don't usually snap at people who've helped me. I apologize."

He nodded.

"Lisa!" Bryan was at her side. "Thank heaven that's over. Are you all right?"

"Yes, I'm fine. Are we still having lunch?"

"I've got to get right over to the hospital. Can I put you in a cab? I'm very sorry."

She let him steer her toward the down side of the escalator.

The manager followed. "I'm so gratified that this turned out so well, madam. Are you certain there are no medical problems? Dr. Cooper here assured me you would be all right ..."

"I'm fine."

"That is such a relief. Now, if you'd like us to have your bracelet repaired —"

Bryan seized on it, and began making the arrangements for having it done.

Glancing over her shoulder, Lisa saw Steve standing at the top of the upward moving escalator, watching her. What was it she saw in his face? Regret? Remorse?

She faced the down escalator with trepidation. She nearly asked Bryan if they could just take the stairs, or the elevator at the far end of the mezzanine, but then she would have to walk past Steve.

She took a deep breath and stepped onto the top tread as it sank before her.

CHAPTER TWO

Lisa sat on Mindy Rollins's sofa, leafing through her friend's portfolio.

"These are really good!" Lisa smiled at her with enthusiasm, and Mindy swallowed hard, as if relieved.

"Do you think so? Because I'd like to break into the art department, but I'm not sure I'm ready."

Mindy had been Clark Media's receptionist for two years. She had told Lisa of her dreams of working as an artist at the upscale advertising agency. Financial stress had forced her to cut her art studies short. She'd dropped out of school, but hadn't given up hope. Landing the job at Clark Media's front desk had kept that hope alive.

Since Lisa started working at Clark three months ago, Mindy had befriended her. Her initial hesitance had puzzled Lisa, until she realized that Mindy considered her to be in a different professional class and was not certain the new art director would socialize with her. But Lisa had warmed to her immediately, and had found that they had much in common. Now Mindy was her closest friend in the office; in the city, for that matter. Not counting Bryan, of course.

A week had passed since the embarrassing escalator incident. Lisa was trying to forget it. The jeweler had called the day before, leaving a message on her voice mail. The bracelet was ready. She knew she ought to pick it up that afternoon, but she dreaded it. Drinking tea with Mindy and looking at her sketches was much more enjoyable.

She hadn't seen Bryan all week. Tonight was their weekly dinner date, provided no emergencies at the hospital intervened, and she ought to be wearing the bracelet, with all fifteen charms intact, when she met him at the Red Jacket.

From Mindy's kitchen came the sound of someone opening and slamming cupboard doors. Lisa jumped and looked toward her hostess. She had never been to Mindy's house before, and assumed she lived alone.

"My brother. He worked late last night." Mindy calmly refilled Lisa's teacup.

Lisa nodded. "You never told me."

"Didn't I?"

"Mindy! We got any milk?" He sounded grouchy and a little sleepy. From the corner of her eye, Lisa had an impression of a scruffy man filling the kitchen doorway, unruly brown hair, a dark stubble on his chin, ragged jeans, white T-shirt, bare feet. She turned away and studied Mindy's portfolio.

"Try the fridge."

More foraging noises.

Lisa turned a page. "Oh, sweet. I love this sketch of the babies."

"That's actually a little boy I used to baby sit. I drew him twice, so it looks like twins."

"Has the mother seen it?"

"Yes, she wanted to buy it, but I made a copy for her."

"Well, if we have an opening, I will definitely consider a résumé from you."

Mindy beamed. "Thanks. I wanted to mention it to you now because, when the time comes, I don't want you to think you have to interview me just because we're friends."

"I'm glad you showed me your stuff. I had no idea you were so talented."

"Do you think I'd have a chance? I mean, most of the artists they hire have degrees, don't they?"

"Talent is more important."

A sharp buzzing noise began in the background. Mindy seemed not to notice it.

"Excuse me, what's that sound?"

"Oh, he's shaving."

Lisa nodded. "Say, there's an art show opening on Gold Street tomorrow. It's Daniel Hubbard. You know, that guy who used to work for Clark Media, then went off on his own as a painter."

"Oh, yeah, yeah. He left before I started there, but everyone talks about him. We've still got some of his framed ads displayed at the office. I'd love to see his new work." Mindy's eyes glowed.

"So go with me."

"Tomorrow?"

"Yes."

"Well, my brother and I usually go to church."

"After lunch. Two o'clock?"

"All right. Want me to come to your apartment?"

"Sure." Lisa drank the last of her tea. "I'd better get going."

"Why don't you come to church with us?" Mindy asked.

Lisa hesitated. "I've visited a couple of churches since I came here, but I've been hoping Bryan would help me decide on one. And the last few weeks, I confess I've just been lazy."

"Come with us."

"*Us* being you and your brother?"

"Yes, and Mrs. Carpenter downstairs. She always rides with us."

"I don't know."

"Mrs. Carpenter doesn't bite, and my brother may bark and growl, but he doesn't either."

Lisa wavered another instant, but the thought of having her best friend along when she visited a new church appealed to her. "All right, if you're sure he won't mind."

"Great." Mindy's smile would have lit the whole of Portland's waterfront. "If you don't like it, I won't pressure you to come back."

"Should I meet you here? What time?"

"Nine thirty?"

"I'll be here." Lisa picked up her purse. "Thanks so much, Mindy. I've got an errand to run now."

"The bracelet?"

"Yes." Lisa had confided in Mindy about her mortifying experience, but hadn't told her of her doubts about her relationship with Bryan.

Mindy grinned. "Thanks for coming. And we'll hit the Hubbard opening after lunch."

"Can we sneak away for lunch after church, just the two of us? Or do you have to come home and cook for your brother?" Lisa walked slowly toward the door.

"No, he can fend for himself."

"Who can?"

Both women turned toward him as he entered the room, and Lisa froze.

He was clean-shaven, his uniform was crisp, and his hair was as casual and fluffy as it had been the week before. Bryan's hadn't looked that good even on the day they'd gone sailing, when the wind had whipped it into disarray. And he had combed it into fastidious neatness again the minute they'd left the boat.

"He cleans up pretty good, doesn't he?" Mindy said in mock surprise. "Steve, this is my friend, Lisa Archer."

"Lisa." He stood looking at her, smiling faintly.

Lisa felt the blood rushing to her cheeks.

"I—I think we've met." She glanced at Mindy.

"You have? When? You didn't tell me!"

"Oh, this *charming* lady and I spent some time together at the mall last week," Steve said lightly.

Lisa wanted to kick his shins, or make a face at him, at least. Instead, she told Mindy, "Your brother is the one who extricated my bracelet from the escalator."

Mindy's jaw dropped. "Stephen! Why didn't you say so? Lisa told me she almost lost her arm in an escalator, but you never said boo!"

Steve shrugged. "I had no idea she was your friend. Besides, we had that big pileup on the highway that night, and the bracelet adventure sort of slipped my mind."

So, he'd forgotten her the minute he left the mall. Lisa realized she had thought about the flippant EMT all week, trying over and over to banish him from her mind. *I've probably thought about him as much as I have about Bryan. Maybe more.*

It wasn't that she was attracted to him. *It's the contrast,* she told herself. *I've worn blinders for three years, never once letting myself admit there were other men out there who might attract me if I'd stop obsessing over Bryan. And then, at the moment I finally face the fact that Bryan maybe isn't the man for me after all, this—this—good-looking churl has to show up.*

She scolded herself mentally. He hadn't been exactly churlish. And she hadn't been her most civil, either.

"Well, I'd better be going." Lisa reached for the doorknob. She was finding the second encounter with Steve Rollins more embarrassing than the first, and she wanted to put distance between them as quickly as possible.

"Be here at 9:30," Mindy reminded her.

"Oh, I—" Lisa turned back, avoiding Steve's eyes. "Maybe I'd better take a rain check."

"No. Come on. We had the whole day planned. Church, then lunch, and the opening." Mindy looked terribly hurt.

"Problem?" Steve asked innocuously.

"I—no. Well—"

"Don't change your plans on account of me."

Lisa's blush deepened, and it infuriated her.

"Your boyfriend's busy this weekend?" He asked, opening a coat closet and reaching for his uniform jacket.

"I—no." She thought for an instant she hated him. She wanted to scream, *None of your business,* but she couldn't, for

Mindy's sake. "We're going out tonight." She looked down at the rug.

Steve turned his facetious smile on her. "Tomorrow's Washington's Birthday. Maybe he'll buy you a little gold hatchet."

Her eyes snapped up to his deep brown ones. His *mocking* deep brown ones. She couldn't believe he was talking to her like this.

"Oh, Steve, you're awful!" Mindy cried. "How can you make fun of Lisa? You don't even know her!"

Lisa felt her bottom lip tremble, and she closed her mouth firmly. She would not cry in front of this baboon.

"'Bye," was all she could manage to Mindy. She rushed out to her car. She didn't feel like picking up the bracelet. It had seemed so heavy lately. She would tell Bryan it wasn't ready yet. No, that would be a lie. She would simply say she hadn't picked it up yet. She turned the ignition key and put the heater on, heading toward home.

***

Mindy began pummeling her brother with her fists the moment the door closed behind Lisa.

"How could you be so rude? That was inexcusable! Lisa was terribly insulted!"

"Hey, hey, leave me alone," he growled, trying to zip his jacket.

"No, I will not leave you alone. I've never seen you be so mean to anyone before."

"I wasn't mean. I was teasing."

"Teasing? You don't know her. You can't tease people you just met. Especially about something as personal as—"

"As what?" He scowled at her. "As her clunky charm bracelet? She hates it. She told me so."

Mindy drew back and stared at him. "She couldn't have been serious. She cherishes that bracelet. It has all those dear little charms for every important thing they've done together."

"Except get engaged, I take it."

Mindy's eyes narrowed. "What are you saying?"

"Nothing. I just got the impression last week that things aren't so peachy between Lovely Lisa and Dr. Charming. She made it very clear to me that he is not her fiancé. What does that say to you?"

Mindy closed the closet door thoughtfully. "You think she was hinting something?"

"To me? No. I just happened to stumble into the emotional maelstrom, I think. She would have told a bus driver or a manicurist. But it was very important to her to say it just then: *He's not my fiancé.*"

Mindy was clearly troubled. "Funny. I thought he was. I mean, she doesn't have a ring or anything, but they've been dating for years, and she wears that bracelet every time they go out. I almost expected her to have a diamond after Valentine's Day."

"Yeah? Well, maybe she expected it, too. She got another cute little charm instead."

"That's awful. It makes what you said even worse."

He tried not to, but he was beginning to feel prickles of compunction. "I've got to get to work," he muttered.

"It's early."

"I know. I'm working a double today."

"Oh, Steve. You'll sleep through church tomorrow. And Lisa was going to go with us, but now she's so mad at you, she won't go."

That blow connected. "I'm sorry. I shouldn't have—" He ran his hand through his hair. "Look, it threw me off balance, seeing her again. I didn't expect it. If I'd known last week she was your friend—"

"You knew today."

He had no answer. "I'll see you in the morning."

He closed the door firmly behind him and went to his pickup truck. The windshield was layered with ice. He started the engine, got the scraper, and viciously attacked the windshield.

Mindy was right. What had made him lash out at Lisa like that, knowing his words would cut deep? Was it because she had hastily declined Mindy's invitation when she found out he was part of the picture? Or because she found the colorless doctor so fascinating, but couldn't bother to look at *him*? Was a doctor worth ten EMTs?

I blew it, he admitted to himself. He got in the truck and drove toward the fire station. That doctor was a fool. Steve knew that if a woman like Lisa loved him, he would have a diamond on her finger faster than you could say cardiovascular.

***

The food at the Red Jacket was excellent, as usual. It was the third time Bryan had taken her there. The hostess knew him by name, or maybe it was just that he'd made a reservation, Lisa wasn't sure.

"How was your week?" Lisa asked. He had called her only once, and then the conversation had been short.

"Hectic. I'm exhausted."

"I'm sorry. We'll make it an early night."

"No, we haven't seen each other for—well, last week hardly counts, does it? Quite a memorable Valentine's Day." Bryan cut a small piece from the end of his steak.

"I'm trying to forget it."

"Is your wrist all right?"

"It's fine." She held it out for display.

"Where's the bracelet?"

"Oh, I haven't got it back yet."

"It was supposed to be ready by the end of the week."

"Yes, they called, but I—I haven't been over to get it yet." She'd almost said *I didn't have time.* Since when had she wanted to lie to Bryan? Was it only since this afternoon?

"Just let me know when you've got it back. Make sure everything's right before you take it out of the store. It's quite an investment."

"Yes." She wondered how big a diamond he could have bought with all that money. Not that she wanted a huge one.

"Bryan?"

"Yes?" He glanced up from his salad.

"I've been thinking maybe I shouldn't wear it so much. I mean, all that gold. You're right about it being valuable, and it's getting cumbersome."

"Cumbersome?"

"Well, you saw what happened on the escalator."

"That was a freak accident."

"Yes, but—well, I've stopped wearing it to work. It gets in the way. I thought maybe I'd put it in a safe deposit box for a while." She didn't tell him that she never wore it except when she knew he would see it.

"But, Lisa, I thought you enjoyed wearing it."

"I did," she said quickly. "I do."

There. She had lied to him. It struck her full in the face.

"Well, I suppose it makes sense not to wear it to the office. But you don't need to put it away."

"But what if someone stole it?"

"Well, it's not *that* valuable."

"Isn't it?" She knew the charms cost at least fifty dollars each. She had no idea how much the bracelet itself was worth. "It's the most expensive piece of jewelry I own, by far."

"For now."

"What do you mean?"

He smiled. "Just that someday you'll have other things, too."

"What kind of things?"

"Oh, I don't know, whatever you like."

She tried to fit what he was saying with his actions.

"When?"

His eyebrows shot up. "Come, Lisa! You want more jewelry? I thought you were a woman of simple taste."

"I guess I am. So what did you mean about all these other jewels I would have?"

He stared at her, a look of incomprehension locked on his face. "Did I miss something?"

"Maybe. Or maybe I did. Bryan, I want to go home."

He looked down at their plates. "We're not finished."

"I'm not hungry."

"Well, I am." He took another bite of steak.

"Excuse me." She stood up.

Bryan swallowed quickly. "Where are you going?"

"I really want to leave."

"In a minute."

"Give me the car keys. I'll wait outside."

"Lisa, it's dark. You're being unreasonable. Sit down." He glanced over his shoulder.

She looked hard at him for a few seconds. The look he returned was just as hard. She knew she couldn't stay in the restaurant another moment.

She turned and walked quickly out of the dining room, to the hostess's desk in the foyer.

"Excuse me, could you please call a cab for me, right away?"

"Yes, ma'am."

Lisa got her coat and put it on. When she turned toward the door, Bryan was in her path.

"What's gotten into you?" He glared at her, his face crimson.

Lisa took a deep breath. "I wasn't trying to make you angry. I just can't discuss this in public. I've asked for a cab."

He stared at her, his jaw working. "All right, if you insist, we'll leave now. Just let me pay for the meal, please?" There was a hard edge to his voice, but Lisa felt she owed him something.

"All right. I'll cancel the cab."

He drove silently out of the parking lot. Lisa was silent, too, except for the catch in her breathing. She found herself praying inwardly, something she hadn't been doing much lately.

"Bryan." It was little more than a whisper, but his expensive car was quiet, and he heard.

"You're actually going to talk to me?"

"Yes, I need to. I'm sorry I made a scene."

He sighed shortly and shook his head. "I don't understand you."

"I don't understand me, either. I lied to you in there, Bryan. I've never, ever done that before, and it scared me."

He said nothing, and that frightened her, too.

After a few seconds, he put the turn signal on and pulled the car into the parking lot of a closed convenience store, threw the gearshift in park, and turned to face her.

"Lisa, what is going on?"

"Just what I said. I lied to you. I'm very sorry." Tears pooled in her eyes, and she blinked rapidly. "I didn't intend to, but you asked me about the bracelet, and I didn't have the courage to tell you the truth."

"The truth? What? They lost the bracelet? What?"

She shook her head. "No, not that. I said I liked wearing it. I don't, Bryan. I used to, but I don't now. It's heavy and awkward and distracting."

She stopped. His expression hadn't changed. Maybe she hadn't really said it out loud.

Very slowly, he cocked his head to one side. "You don't like the bracelet anymore?"

She sighed and leaned her head back against the headrest. "Bryan, listen to me. It's not about the bracelet."

"It's not? Okay, it's not."

He was confused, she could see that. Was she being that cryptic? Surely anyone who could get A's in anatomy and physiology could figure this out.

"How do you feel about me?"

He hesitated. "You mean right now, or in general?"

"Oh, Bryan, there's no wrong answer. I just want to know. How do you feel about me? Do you love me?"

He looked down toward the dim lights of the dashboard. "Well, of course."

"Not *of course*. How could it be *of course*? How am I supposed to know this?"

"I thought…there wasn't any wrong answer. I found one, didn't I?"

She felt guiltier than ever.

"Look, Bryan, I'm sorry to put you through this. I've been feeling lately that we're not as…compatible…as I once thought we were. The bracelet is just one of a thousand things we don't' agree on."

"It *is* about the bracelet," he insisted.

"No, it's not. It's about the ring."

He sat back, leaning against the door, eyeing her warily. After a moment he said quietly, "What ring?"

"That's it precisely. You said in there I'd have lots of jewelry someday, but I don't want that. I just want a loving, faithful husband."

He swallowed. "This is getting complicated."

"No, it's simple. Do you want to marry me? Or do you want to go on taking me out to dinner once a week forever, and buying me a new charm every couple of months? Speak now, or forever hold your peace. But I'll warn, you, I've waited so long that I'm not likely to believe you unless it's pretty convincing."

She was breathing fast, and shaking a little. She knew that whatever happened in the next two minutes would alter the course of her life.

Bryan clenched his fists on the steering wheel, staring out through the windshield.

"So. It's not about the bracelet."

"Right."

"Lisa, What do you want?"

It was half a chuckle and half a sigh that came out. *What do I want?* she thought. *I want you to throw your arms around me and pledge your undying love—and mean it. I want you to take me to city hall tomorrow for a marriage license. I want you to cherish me every day of your life.*

Wearily, she said, "Just take me home, Bryan. You can pick the bracelet up at the jeweler's anytime."

He moved in slow motion, turning on the lights, putting the car in gear. But when he stepped on the gas pedal, everything went too fast. They plunged out onto the street. Lisa saw that the approaching beer truck couldn't stop.

"Bryan!" She threw her hands in front of her face.

CHAPTER THREE

"10-55 on High Street, looks bad," the dispatcher called from his tiny office at the fire station. "Steve and Jimmy, get going. Bud and Hank, Unit 2."

It had been a quiet evening up to that point, so quiet that Steve had accepted Jimmy's challenge for a game of chess. But they had never made it through an entire game, and they wouldn't tonight, either.

The checklist was performed quickly. Jimmy drove, and Steve buckled into the passenger seat. The siren screamed, muffled by the sound-deadening lining in the cab.

"What a way to spend Saturday night," Jimmy said, turning onto High Street.

"Got nothing better to do," Steve replied.

"What, there's no girl you'd like to be out with right now?"

"Well, when you put it that way…But she wouldn't want to be with me."

"Why not?" Jimmy had a sunny disposition, and girls liked him. He couldn't understand Steve, who pushed women away with his moodiness.

"I made her mad," Steve said glumly. "Said something I shouldn't have."

"So apologize. Send flowers. Better yet, hand deliver them."

"I don't think so. Not for this girl."

Jimmy laughed. "You don't know much about women, do you? They all love flowers."

Steve spotted the wreckage in the road ahead—a white beer truck turned on its side, and the remains of a small silver sports car smashed between it and a brick wall. He reached for the radio and called in their position.

As soon as Jimmy had the ambulance stopped, Steve hopped out with his bag and ran toward the car. A small crowd had gathered, and a bystander was trying to open the driver's door.

"How many?" Steve asked.

"There's two in here, and one guy in the truck," a balding man told him. "We can't get this door open."

"All right, thank you, sir. Just stand back. We'll see what we can do."

Jimmy was beside him. "Bud and Hank are getting the truck driver. What do we need?"

"Jaws of Life, I'm thinking." Steve pulled futilely at the door handle.

"Try the other side," Jimmy said.

"Don't know as we can get between the car and the wall."

"I can." Before Steve could stop him, Jimmy scrambled over the smashed roof.

"This door's unlocked. I don't know if I can open it wide enough. If we could tow the car a couple of feet, I could get the woman out. That would be faster than cutting the roof off."

"All right," Steve said. "Can you get her vitals?"

"I think so. Hold on."

Steve bent down and looked in the driver's window. A man lay slumped over the wheel, with blooding oozing down his cheek. His arms hung limp. Steve pressed the button on the radio strapped to his shoulder.

"We need backup here, and a tow truck stat."

Two police cruisers arrived, announced by shrill sirens and flashing blue lights.

"I think she's conscious," Jimmy yelled. "Pulse 120. Reps 24. I can't get the BP yet."

"Obvious injuries?"

"Hold on."

Jimmy ducked his head back into the passenger compartment.

Bud came up behind Steve. "We've got our patient, and we're heading for the hospital. There's a tow truck and another bus on the way."

"Right. Thanks."

"Hey, Steve!" Jimmy shouted.

"What?"

"She looks like that lady at the mall. You know, the one with the stupid bracelet?"

"Lisa?" Steve sucked in air. They couldn't wait for the tow truck.

"You fellows need some help?" A burly, bearded man had detached himself from the spectators.

"Yes. Get a couple of those cops and help us move this car a little, so we can get the other door open all the way."

With four other men, Steve and Jimmy managed to wrestle the crushed car away from the wall. Jimmy swung the passenger door wide, but Steve pushed in beside him.

A cold wave washed over him. It was Lisa. She might detest him, but he would do anything in his power to help her.

"Lisa! Lisa, can you hear me?"

***

She opened her eyes and tried to focus.

"Bryan?"

Her fantasy was coming true. He had thrown his arms around her after all, and was sobbing her name in shattered tones of penitence and love.

"Lisa, what hurts? Tell me what hurts."

Tender hands were unstrapping her seat belt and lifting her. She tried to put her arm up around Bryan's neck, but that was too hard, so she let it fall back.

He was carrying her. This couldn't be. Never in her wildest imaginings had Bryan carried her anywhere Rhett Butler style, not even over the threshold.

"Bryan?"

He lowered her gently onto something—a bed—no, something like a bed.

"Lisa, you've been in an accident. We're taking you to the hospital. Lisa, do you hear me?"

She nodded. Opening her eyes again, she tried to look at him, but bright lights were flashing, and she squeezed her eyelids tight shut again.

She was moving. She grabbed wildly for something to hold on to and found a metal rail. It hurt when she squeezed it. "Bryan!" she gasped.

"It's okay, ma'am," an unfamiliar voice said, near her right ear. "We're getting him. Just take it easy."

Her head ached. A loud wailing went on and on. Every breath hurt.

"Lisa."

That voice wasn't Bryan's. It was deeper, but she knew it. Or she ought to.

"Lisa, can you hear me?"

"Yes."

"Atta girl. I'm going to start an IV line in your hand. It may hurt a little. Do you understand?"

She didn't. She opened her eyes. The man from the escalator was bending close to her. Steve Something. Mindy's jerk of a brother. Did he have his wire cutters? He had such great hair. Pain stabbed at her right hand. The bracelet was cutting into her. She was moving again. The escalator had started, and her hand was being pulled into it. She tried to scream, but only a low moan escaped.

***

Steve stood slouched against the wall in the corridor outside the emergency room. She'd been in there half an hour, then over to X-ray, and was back in the ER now. A woman like that ought to have family out here waiting and praying.

Her identification had listed a woman two thousand miles away as her next of kin. When he'd called, she'd told him she was Lisa's sister. She couldn't come tonight but would fly out in the morning. Would Lisa be all right?

He tried to think who else he could call.

Well, there was Dr. Bryan Charming for starters. Only he was up in surgery.

Who else?

Mindy. He ought to call Mindy. Lisa was Mindy's friend.

He pushed away from the wall and fumbled for his cell phone. It rang four times before Mindy answered, groggy.

"Mindy, it's Steve. I'm at the hospital. We just brought in some patients from a car wreck."

"Uh-huh."

She didn't sound awake yet.

"Mindy, one of the victims is Lisa."

"Oh, no!"

"Yeah. Lisa and her boyfriend, the doctor. What's his name?"

"Bryan Cooper?"

"That's the guy. He's pretty bad. Lisa's hurt, too. Do you want to come over here? She's got nobody, Mindy."

"I'll come."

"Good. Look for me in the ER."

Jimmy came out from the nurses' station as he put away his phone. "They said she's stable. You ready to roll?"

"No, I want to stay. Jimmy, I called my sister. That Lisa Archer is Mindy's best friend."

"You're kidding."

"No, I didn't know it last week when she got her bracelet stuck in the escalator, but I met her this morning. She came over to the apartment to see Mindy."

Jimmy whistled.

"We've only got an hour left on this shift. I want to stay here," Steve insisted.

"Sure. I'll tell Jack it's a personal friend."

"Thanks, buddy. So, flowers, you think?"

Jimmy looked at him critically. "Don't tell me she's the girl you made mad."

Steve shrugged. "It was just something stupid I said."

"Man, she's got a boyfriend upstairs in critical condition."

"I know."

Jimmy clapped him on the shoulder. "Maybe flowers isn't enough in this case."

"What do you suggest?"

"Well, she likes clunky jewelry."

Steve smiled. "No, I don't think I'll offer her any jewelry just yet."

"Well, a sympathetic shoulder might be in order, especially if the boyfriend croaks."

Steve winced. "You're right. I should just apologize, then get out of her life."

"Seems like a wise move to me." Jimmy sauntered toward the door of the ambulance bay, but turned back. "Of course, Miss Archer is an exceptional lady. If you think you have a chance, I'd say spring for flowers *and* jewelry."

When the door closed behind Jimmy, Steve went purposefully to the nurses' station.

"Hi, Jimmy says Lisa Archer is stable now?"

"Yes, she has a sprained wrist, a slight concussion, and some bruising from the seat belt, but everything seems okay internally. We're going to keep her overnight."

"I reached her sister in Nebraska. She'll be here tomorrow."

"No parents?" the nurse asked.

"Apparently not. This girl is a friend of my sister's, though, and I called her. She's coming in. Will she be able to see Miss Archer?"

"Probably. They're moving her upstairs now."

"What room?"

"321."

He nodded. Two nurses were rolling a gurney out of an exam room, and he could see Lisa's blonde hair fanned out on the pillow. "My sister's name is Mindy Rollins. If she comes in here asking for Miss Archer, will you give her the room number?"

"Certainly."

He followed the gurney to the elevator.

When Lisa was settled in the room, he sat down in the armchair beside the bed. The nurses accepted him without question as a family friend and let him stay, even though it was long past visiting hours. His uniform helped, he was sure.

He sat watching her face. Her skin was normally pale, but it was chalky now. Her hair framed her face in a dark golden cloud. He knew from years of experience that accident victims seldom looked their best, but even so, Lisa was beautiful. Not the flawless, sculptured beauty that would win a pageant, but the natural grace and vulnerability that had sideswiped him the week before, when he'd seen her woefully waiting, handcuffed to a stairway.

If it weren't for Bryan Cooper…but that line of thought wouldn't help. He began to pray silently for Lisa, thankful that her injuries were comparatively minor.

Then he prayed for Bryan. It was difficult at first, but Bryan was badly injured, and Steve was dedicated to helping those in need. He wondered what Bryan was really like. What kind of man would a girl like Lisa choose? When it came right down to it, what did he really know about Lisa?

He realized in an instant that he had not been honest when he'd said he had forgotten her. All week long she had been in the back of his mind. In their brief meeting at the mall, she had seemed decent, emotionally wounded, but solid somehow. Her dress, her demeanor, everything about her had made him feel that she was the kind of girl he would seek out if he knew where to find her. Why, then, had he spoken to her as he had today, with sarcasm and taunting?

He slid down in the chair and talked to God without words. It would take supernatural power to straighten out the tangle of emotions and hurt he had stirred up.

Her hand fluttered, and Steve sat up, leaning closer.

"Lisa?"

Her eyelashes lifted slowly, exposing green eyes. She flicked a glance to his face, then closed them again.

"Lisa, can you hear me? You've been injured. You're in the hospital."

Slowly, her eyelids went up again.

"Bryan," she whispered.

"He's hurt, too. They're taking care of him."

She swallowed with effort.

"Would you like some water?"

She nodded.

He reached for the glass of ice water on the night table, and put the end of the bent straw to Lisa's lips.

She sipped at it, then collapsed into the pillow.

"Thank you."

"You're welcome."

He watched her intently. Her long, fine eyelashes drooped toward her cheeks.

"Lisa. Stay with me here."

Her eyes flew open. She looked confused for an instant, then focused on him.

"Steve…right?"

"Yes. My partner and I responded to the accident."

"So, you rescued me again."

He made a face. "Listen, I'm sorry about what I said earlier."

"What did you say?"

"About the charm bracelet."

"Oh, that." Her eyelids closed again.

"Are you asleep?" he asked anxiously.

"No." It was a whisper, but distinct. "Forget about the bracelet. It's nothing to me. I don't have it anymore."

He sat still, unable to make anything of her words. At last he asked, "Where is it?"

She didn't answer. Her breathing was gentle and shallow. He sat for another ten minutes, hardly moving, watching her with wistful longing, wishing he could comfort her.

There were footsteps at the door. He looked up and saw Mindy peering in at him, her face strained.

"Is she okay?"

He stood and strode to the doorway.

"Concussion, sprained wrist, bruising. They think she'll be all right, but they're monitoring her. She's been conscious a few minutes. She was talking to me."

"What did she say?" Mindy's fear had tempered to concern, and she watched Lisa as she questioned him.

He hesitated. "She knew me. I apologized for—you know, this morning, and she said to forget it. And she said she doesn't have the bracelet anymore."

Mindy stared at him. "That can't be right. She was going to pick it up from the jeweler's this afternoon."

He shrugged. "Maybe it wasn't ready, or maybe she's not thinking clearly, but that's what she said."

Or maybe she had given it back to Bryan. He wondered if one gold charm bracelet was in the bag of personal effects they had collected in the emergency room.

Mindy pushed past him and walked to the bedside. Steve followed and stood behind his sister, looking over her shoulder at Lisa. She was utterly defenseless.

In that moment, Steve appointed himself her defender.

"Lisa?" Mindy said. "Lisa, are you all right, honey?"

Lisa blinked and searched for the voice. When she found Mindy's face, she smiled.

"Mindy! Hi!" It was barely more than a moan.

Mindy grasped her friend's hand. "Hello! How you doing?"

"I'm not sure. I think I'm sick."

"No, honey, you were in a car accident. Steve and Jimmy brought you to the hospital in the ambulance. Do you remember the ambulance?"

"No, but I was on the escalator and—" Lisa halted, perplexed. "Is Bryan here?"

"He's in another room, Lisa. He's hurt."

She frowned and closed her eyes. Mindy looked around at Steve.

"Does she know?"

"I tried to tell her."

"How bad is it?" Lisa whispered. Her eyes were open again, and she was staring at Steve. "Tell me."

He moved in close, leaning on the bed rail, until he was sure she was looking into his eyes.

"Lisa, Bryan is hurt badly. They took him to surgery."

"What—what is it?"

"Liver and spleen. He had a head injury, too, and one leg was broken." He spoke slowly, quietly.

Lisa's eyebrows knit as she absorbed what he was saying. She reached toward him feebly.

"Could you ..."

"What?" Steve asked. He caught her hand and held it. Her cool fingers clasped his with more strength than he'd anticipated. "Could I what?"

" ...ask?"

"Sure. Mindy will stay with you. I'll go check on him."

She closed her eyes.

Mindy's anxiety poured from her face. She whispered, "Are you sure she's going to be okay?"

"The doctor says so. She's medicated now. I think you'll see a big improvement in the morning."

Mindy nodded. "Well, if you want to go check on Bryan, I'll sit with her."

He went out into the hallway and stopped at the nurses' desk.

"Can I check on the patient, Bryan Cooper?"

"Doctor Cooper is still in surgery."

"Where?"

She told him, and he went down a floor on the elevator, to the surgery waiting area. The charge nurse there was more helpful.

"His surgeon just came out. You can catch him in the locker room. Dr. Mason."

Steve went without pause into the doctors' locker room.

"Dr. Mason?"

"Yes?" The graying man was changing his clothes, and he seemed annoyed at the interruption.

"I'm Steve Rollins. I was with one of the ambulance crews that brought in the accident victims tonight."

"Yes?"

"We've got Dr. Cooper's fiancée—well, his girlfriend—upstairs." *He's not my fiancé.* Steve shoved that memory away. "She's conscious now, and asking about him. What news can I take her?"

"Upstairs?"

The doctor seemed rather stupid to Steve.

"Yes, sir. She's concussed. They're monitoring her overnight."

"Then to whom, may I ask, did I just give a report?"

"I've no idea, sir."

"Red-haired woman in the family waiting area. Pretty, high heels, heavy makeup."

Steve shook his head blankly.

"You say you brought in his girlfriend?" Dr. Mason asked.

"Yes, sir."

"She told you she was his girlfriend?"

"Yes." Steve was becoming a bit impatient.

"I don't believe it."

"Well, I know this woman and—"

"You know her personally?"

"Yes. Not very well, but I've met her a couple of times."

"And she was injured tonight as well. Was she in the car with Cooper?"

"Yes. I helped take her out at the scene."

Dr. Mason shrugged. "It makes no sense. The woman in the waiting room claimed to be his girlfriend. I told her she can go into the recovery room after they move him."

Steve knew his eyes were bulging. "I see."

"You do? Because I don't." The doctor pulled on a green golf shirt. "But then, it's none of my business. Except that Cooper's an intern here. If his personal life is that messed up, it could affect his work." He glared at Steve. "What am I saying? He won't work for at least six weeks, as it is."

"This woman," Steve said uneasily.

"See for yourself." Dr. Mason slammed his locker door. "I'm going home and go to bed."

"But Dr. Cooper will recover?"

"Oh yes, in time. He's got a rod in his ankle, and a lacerated liver. He'll make it, though."

Steve followed the doctor slowly into the hallway and watched him get on the elevator. He spotted a sign that read Family Waiting Area, and went to the doorway.

She sat on the edge of one of the green vinyl chairs, leafing through a magazine. High heels, all right, and legs a mile long. Steve made his eyes skip over the short skirt to her face. Definitely more sophisticated than Lisa Archer. The makeup was well done, but showy. It drew attention to her full lips, her plucked and penciled brows, her hollow cheeks. No one feature stood out as her best. Her hair, a shade brighter than auburn, gleamed in the fluorescent lighting.

She looked up suddenly, and started to rise, then sat back down, appraising him.

He nodded toward her impersonally and left.

In the elevator, he leaned back against the wall.

What do I tell Lisa? This is a huge mess. What on earth do I tell her?

CHAPTER FOUR

When he arrived at the hospital after church Sunday, Mindy was alone in Room 321. Steve's heart raced as he looked quickly around the room and noted the open bathroom door.

"Where is she?"

"Lisa? She went down the hall to see Bryan."

"No. She can't."

"Why not?"

He looked at his sister, then away from her piercing eyes. Mindy had gone to Lisa's apartment that morning to get her friend a change of clothes, and Steve had gone to church with Mrs. Carpenter.

"Her doctor signed her out twenty minutes ago," Mindy said. "They put Bryan in a room down the hall in the middle of the night, and she wanted to see him. I told her I'd pack her things for her while she went."

"She went down there alone?"

"Well, yeah. She just left a second ago. She's a lot better, Steve, really. I know she looked awful last night, but a lot of that was the medication." Mindy's frown deepened. "Do you know something about Bryan that I don't? Is his condition worse than you let on last night?"

"No, I just—maybe I should go down there and make sure she's all right."

"I've got her things ready. I'll go with you."

"You don't have to. I'll get Lisa and meet you downstairs."

"Steve, what is the matter with you? She's my best friend."

"I know."

"So, let's go."

Steve took the blue overnight bag from her, and they walked past the nurses' desk and down the hallway, past a girl shelving trays of dirty dishes on a large cart. Each step was harder as his dread increased.

When they approached the door of 306, he stopped, his hand on Mindy's arm.

"Why don't I just peek in there?"

Mindy opened her mouth to reply, her face in a puzzled scowl, when Lisa Archer came swiftly out of Room 306, her face pale. She didn't look at them, but went straight across to the elevator and punched the down button hard, then leaned with one hand against the wall, her head bowed.

"Lisa!" Mindy rushed after her, but Steve hung back. The look on Lisa's face was one of anguish.

He strode to the door of 306 and looked in. Bryan Cooper was ensconced in the bed, tubes and cords tethering him to a variety of apparatus. His eyes were closed, his face nearly as white as the pillowcase.

Beyond the bed, the red-haired woman was standing, staring toward Steve. She had a slightly bewildered air, but didn't seem unduly troubled.

"Hello," she said uncertainly.

"Excuse me. A young woman just left here."

"Yes. She said she was a friend of my fiancé's, but I don't know her."

He nodded. "Sorry for bothering you."

He backed out of the room, leaving her with an even more baffled expression.

The elevator door opened. Lisa stepped stiffly into the car and turned to face the door, staring straight ahead. Mindy boarded and stood beside her.

"Lisa, dear, what is it? Is Bryan all right? Do we need to speak to his doctor?"

Steve hesitated. He didn't want to upset her even more with his presence. Maybe he should let the elevator go and catch the next one.

Mindy saw him hanging back and put her hand out to stop the door from closing.

"Come on, Steve."

He got into the car and stood facing the control panel without looking at Lisa.

"Lisa?" Mindy was solicitous, but her friend still did not look at her. "Can we do anything for you?"

"Just take me home, please." Lisa's voice was brittle.

Mindy glanced toward Steve. He shrugged and looked back at the control panel. But he knew that once again he was responsible for bringing Lisa pain.

***

"You could have told me!" Mindy was furious.

Steve sighed. How was it he always did the wrong thing where Lisa was concerned?

It had seemed the right course the night before. He had prayed and not had any flashes of revelation, so he had said nothing about the redhead at the hospital. But now Mindy was letting him know that he ought to have done something.

Anything, it seemed, was better than nothing.

He glanced toward the car window. Lisa was sitting in the passenger seat of Mindy's compact staring straight ahead, while he and Mindy stood a few feet away arguing.

"Look, I'm sorry. I wasn't sure what was going on, and I didn't want to upset Lisa. I figured she had enough pain. Why don't you take her home, and we'll talk about this later?"

Mindy scowled at him. "Where did she come from?"

"Who? The redhead? How should I know?"

Still she eyed him distrustfully. "I don't know what you're up to, Stephen, but Lisa's health is what's important right now."

"Exactly. So take her home and put her to bed. I'll see you later."

He watched as Mindy got into the car and spoke to Lisa, but if Lisa replied she didn't move her lips. He headed for his truck, unable to shake the dismal ache in his stomach.

When Mindy arrived home, he was making macaroni and cheese he'd dumped from a cardboard box. He'd figured she would stay with Lisa and he was on his own for lunch. She tossed her tiny purse on the counter and stared at him malevolently.

"Lisa won't talk to me. I hope you're happy."

"No, I'm not happy, but I don't see what I could have done differently."

"If you'd told me last night, maybe I'd have been able to help her this morning. I certainly wouldn't have blithely sent her off to visit Bryan alone."

"I—" Steve gave it up. Mindy took no excuses. "How is she?"

"She said she wants to be alone, and that she'll be all right until her sister gets here. I hated leaving her by herself, but it seems the Rollins family is persona non grata with Lisa right now, so I left her with a sandwich and the phone within reach."

Steve ducked his head and studiously examined the instructions on the macaroni package.

Mindy sat down on a stool by the counter. "I shouldn't have let her go to Bryan's room alone, anyway. I ought to have realized that seeing him all smashed up would be a shock to her. But I had no idea. No idea whatsoever!" She glared pointedly at Steve.

"I'm sorry. I didn't see that telling her would have helped her last night. She was already pretty low."

"You could have clued me in. Then I would have known what she was up against, poor thing!"

He slammed the box onto the counter. "Look, let's be fair. Bryan hasn't told us that woman is anything to him. She told Dr. Mason she was his girlfriend. She told me he's her fiancé. Maybe Bryan doesn't know her from Joan of Arc."

"That's crazy. People don't just move into the hospital and claim accident victims like that. Someone must have called her. She had to be listed as next of kin or something."

Steve thought about that. "I wonder who they did call?"

"A man can't have two fiancées," Mindy insisted.

"He and Lisa were *not* engaged."

"Well, practically."

"You still think so?"

Mindy sighed and began making coffee. Steve got out the milk and margarine and drained the macaroni. They worked silently.

It was while they were eating the salty macaroni that Mindy said, "Lisa must know his family. They've dated for three years."

"I don't know. Maybe he doesn't have a family." Steve sipped his coffee. It was too strong. Mindy never seemed to get it right. One day it was weak as dishwater, the next, strong enough to corrode steel. He poured milk into his mug and stirred it. "Maybe he's had two girlfriends for a long time. One city girl and one hometown girl."

Mindy's eyes glittered. "And when Lisa moved to the city, his two worlds came into dangerous proximity."

"Maybe he's been shuffling them all this time, trying to make sure they never met," Steve agreed. "It's possible."

"But Lisa always talked about him as if he was the sweetest guy on earth."

"Hmm." Sweet was not the word Steve would have used to describe the man who had snapped at him, *That's 18-karat gold, buddy.*

"You said yesterday that you gathered Lisa was having second thoughts about him, but I thought you were jumping to conclusions," Mindy said tentatively.

Steve nodded in surprise. Finally Mindy was ready to listen to him. "At the mall, she sounded like she was emotionally drained. Maybe that's what set me off yesterday. She was so cool. I thought Dr. Charming wasn't as saintly as she would have people believe, but she wouldn't hear a word against him."

"It wasn't your place to say a word against him, Steve. You don't know either of them."

"True." He scraped the last of the macaroni from his plate and reached for the pan.

"Do you think she'll be okay?"

"How should I know? We don't know what that woman said to her." Steve heaped more noodles onto his plate, then looked up at Mindy. "Did you notice anything special about her?"

"Lisa?"

"No, the other one."

"I didn't see her."

"That's right." He frowned, trying to remember every detail.

"You know something." She leaned toward him, her eyes narrowing in accusation.

"She's just—she's not Lisa's type. Very different."

"How?"

"Flamboyant." He shrugged, dissatisfied with the word.

"Tacky?" Mindy asked.

"Well …"

"I'll kill him."

Steve weighed the consequences of telling her more. Better to have Mindy as an ally than to not tell her and reap her wrath later for keeping her in the dark. Maybe the two of them could help Lisa sort things out.

"She had some jewelry," he offered cautiously.

Her eyes widened. "A charm bracelet?"

"No. A ring."

Mindy gasped. "Killing's too good for him."

Steve shook his head, thinking hard. "I didn't see it up close. It might not be a diamond."

"Maybe I'd better go back over to Lisa's apartment."

"I thought she wanted to be alone."

"She does. And I promised I'd pick her sister up at the airport at three." Mindy sighed and picked up her coffee mug. "Yuck!" Her face contorted. "This is awful."

***

At quarter past three, Mindy called from the airport.

"Steve, the plane's delayed. I tried to call Lisa and tell her, but there was no answer."

"So what do you want me to do?"

"Go over and see if Lisa's okay."

"Oh, no, I'm not suicidal."

"Steve, she's ill. She's not answering her phone. I'm stuck here for another hour and a half. You can be at her place in ten minutes. *Please.* Do this for me."

He sighed. "She hates me."

"So? I'll call her apartment again in fifteen minutes. You be there answering the phone."

"I don't think this is—" He stared at the receiver. Mindy had hung up.

CHAPTER FIVE

He knocked softly and waited twenty seconds, then knocked again, louder. Still no response. He wanted to turn away and go home, but Mindy would draw and quarter him if he did.

What if something had happened? She might be in there unconscious. His knocking became hammering. He cared about Lisa, and she needed friends right now, whether she admitted it or not. Maybe she had taken sleeping pills. He had responded to dozens of suicides, intentional or accidental. What if—

The door swung open.

Lisa stood clutching the edge of it. The skin below her green eyes was dark. She looked through him, not at him.

"What do you want?"

"Are you all right?"

"Yes."

"Mindy made me come over. Your sister's plane is delayed, and she couldn't get you on the phone."

Lisa didn't seem to be focusing.

"Are you sure you're all right?" he asked. She leaned on the door jamb, and Steve stepped toward her, expecting her to pitch forward any second. "Lisa, I think you ought to sit down."

She didn't protest as he took her arm and stepped inside, guiding her to a rocking chair. He knelt beside her.

"Breathe, Lisa."

"Leave me alone."

He leaned back away from her, but didn't dare leave her side. She had thrown a housecoat over shorts and a Minnie Mouse T-shirt. Her face was haggard, her eyes closed. He could see blue veins in her eyelids.

After ten seconds, she opened one eye.

"You're still here," she whispered.

"I—I don't really think you should be alone."

"Spoken like an EMT."

"Did you take something?" It was a standard question in his line of work, but it was scary this time.

"Just what they gave me at the hospital."

They ought to have kept her another night. She was badly shaken in the accident, and the emotional explosion was aggravating her physical condition. He reached automatically for her wrist, to take her pulse, but she jerked away from his touch.

"Sorry, I was just—"

The phone rang.

"That will be Mindy," he said. "Do you want me to get it?"

She nodded shortly, and he stood up. The telephone was on an end table beside the puffy blue print sofa.

"Hello."

"Yes, I'm trying to call Lisa Archer. Have I reached the right number?"

Not Mindy. Steve didn't recognize the woman's voice.

"Yes, I'm a friend of Lisa's. May I ask who is calling?"

"This is Sylvia Cooper. I'm calling to see if Lisa is all right. I'm at the hospital, and I understand she was injured last night with my son, Bryan."

"Y-yes. Just a minute, Mrs. Cooper. Let me see if Lisa's up to speaking with you."

He pushed the mute button. Lisa was leaning back in her chair, eyes closed again.

"Lisa, it's Bryan Cooper's mother. His family is at the hospital. Do you want to talk to her?"

Slowly, the long eyelashes went up, revealing her green eyes. "Tell her I'm sorry Bryan is hurt."

Steve hesitated, then spoke into the receiver.

"Mrs. Cooper? Lisa wants me to tell you that she's sorry Bryan is hurt. Have you spoken to his doctor?"

"Yes. He'll recover, but it will take some time."

"Will you be staying in town, ma'am?"

"Well, my husband and I and Bryan's sister are here. We're not really sure what we'll do. I'd like to stay near him for a few days, I think. We were wondering if we could see Lisa."

"Uh, hold on."

He looked at her, and walked slowly to her chair, carrying the receiver.

"Lisa." He put his hand on her shoulder, and her eyes popped open. "Lisa, Mrs. Cooper would like to see you, if you feel up to it."

"No," she whispered.

"You want me to tell her no? Just like that?"

She sighed and reached for the telephone.

"Hello, Sylvia? Yes, yes, it was. They let me go this morning. Oh, I bumped my head and I have some bruises, but it's not too bad. I'm really tired. Thank you." Steve felt she was forcing cheerfulness into her voice.

There was a pause.

"Yes, I looked in on him before I came home. He wasn't awake."

Again she listened, and her face began to crumple. In silence, she held the receiver toward Steve. He took it and held it to her ear. Mrs. Cooper was talking nonstop now.

"—and we just didn't know what to think. She said she was at Bryan's apartment last night when the hospital called. Dear, if you know who she is—"

"Mrs. Cooper," Steve said quietly.

The frantic voice stopped dead.

"Ma'am, Lisa's given the phone back to me. I don't think she can talk anymore."

"Oh." There was a moment's silence. "You're a close friend?"

"No, actually it's my sister, Mindy, who is Lisa's friend, but Mindy has gone to the airport for Lisa's sister, and she asked me to check in on Lisa because of her injuries."

"Oh. I was just asking about this other girl who is here at the hospital. Audra, her name is, apparently, and we've never seen her before, but she seems very chummy with Bryan, but Bryan is heavily medicated, and—oh, dear." The voice stopped.

Steve glanced at Lisa.

"Tell her," Lisa whispered hoarsely, "that I'm very sorry Bryan is in bad shape, but that I'm not going with him anymore. Tell her that, please. And say that I can't see his family. Please. I can't talk to her. I just can't."

Two tears rolled down her face, on each side of her perfect nose.

Steve put his ear back to the receiver. Mrs. Cooper was speaking again.

"I feel so badly about this—Bryan being hurt, and this woman materializing like this, and poor Lisa. Where did they go last night? It's all so—"

"Ma'am," Steve said gently. He wrestled to relay Lisa's message politely. "Lisa says she's concerned about your son, but she is no longer going with him."

"No longer—what does that mean? She was with him last night!"

Steve looked anxiously at Lisa, but she was no help. Her eyes were closed, and she gripped the arms of the rocker, her knuckles white.

"She asked me to say that she's not able to see you, or maybe she just doesn't want to. She really needs to rest, I think."

"They broke up?"

The question crackled into his ear.

"Are you telling me Lisa and Bryan broke up? I really must speak with her again. Heavens, they've gone together for years, and we've known her since she was a little girl. She can't have broken up with him. I consider her my future daughter-in-law. Do you hear me? We *love* Lisa."

"I—I'm sorry, ma'am. That's all she told me, and I don't know the situation. Maybe tomorrow she'll feel better. You might try again then. Good-bye." He hung up and looked toward Lisa. She had slumped down in the rocking chair. If she were sleeping, she might slide out into a heap on the rug.

The phone rang again.

"Stephen?"

"Yes, Mindy, it's me."

"It's about time!"

"Bryan's mother called."

"Oh! Really?"

"Yes, they're at the hospital."

"What did Lisa say?"

"She had me tell her that she and Bryan are no longer an item, and she doesn't want to see them."

For once, Mindy was speechless. Steve groped for the name of Lisa's sister.

"Any word on Minerva?"

"It's Miriam. She'll be here in an hour. Can you stay with Lisa, Steve?"

"I don't think she wants me to, but she's pretty out of it."

"Well, then, I'll come over there, and you come wait for Miriam."

"Oh, come on. Do I have to make explanations to yet another strange woman today?"

"Stephen!"

"All right, come on over here."

He went over to Lisa and put his hands on her shoulders. She looked up at him wearily.

"Lisa, come on, you ought to lie down."

She struggled to get up and swayed.

Steve put his arms around her.

"Just relax. I'll carry you."

"No." She struggled away from him, and stumbled to the couch, flopping down on it.

He followed her and lifted her feet onto the cushions. She stretched out, fumbling for a throw pillow, and he settled one under her head. She turned away from him, toward the back of the couch, and lay there motionless. A tapestry afghan was folded over the back of the sofa. He tugged at it and unfolded it, laying it gently over her.

He went to her bedroom and entered cautiously. Very feminine. Forest green print comforter with matching curtains, nice Renoir print on the wall, and an eight-by-ten of Bryan on the dresser. On the night table, a glass of water and a pill bottle sat by the lamp. He picked up the prescription bottle and read the label, then opened it and counted the pills.

He went back to the living room and sat down on the floor beside her, pushing the coffee table aside with his feet.

So much for being her knight in shining armor.

They also serve who only stand and wait. Or who only sit on the floor and wait. He wasn't sure Milton knew what he was talking about.

After ten minutes, she stirred and rolled over, burrowing into the throw pillows. One arm flopped down over the edge of the couch and bumped his shoulder. He watched her face, but she seemed to be genuinely asleep. Gently, he touched her hand.

"Oh, Lisa. If things could have been different." He held her limp fingers and leaned his temple against the side of the couch. With a start, he realized he'd been counting her respirations without thinking about it. Shallow and fast. He brought his other hand up and felt her pulse, turning his wrist so he could see his watch. He held her hand loosely, not wanting to let go, but not wanting to rouse her, either, to snap at him again. Her golden hair hid part of her face, and he itched to smooth it back from her cheek, but it was too risky. If she woke up to his touch, she would be furious.

Knocking sounded at the door. He got up quietly and went to open it.

"Hi." Mindy peered past him. "How's she doing?"

"Sleeping on the couch."

They walked softly in and stood looking at her. Steve bent and pulled the afghan up to her shoulder.

Lisa's eyes flickered open.

"Go away."

"I'm just leaving. Mindy's here now."

She closed her eyes.

Steve looked at Mindy. Mindy nodded toward the door, and they walked toward it. Steve retrieved his jacket from a chair on the way by.

"I told you she hates me." He zipped the coat and pulled his gloves from the pockets.

"No, she doesn't. She's hurting right now."

"Huh."

"Go get her sister."

Steve gave it one more try. "Do I have to? I haven't been doing so well with the Archer family."

"Just pick her up and bring her here, that's all I ask. And when Lisa feels better and understands how much you've helped, she won't hate you."

He sighed and went out the door.

During the drive to the airport, he went over the events of the past twenty-four hours in his mind. He'd apologized, and Lisa had said *forget about it*, but he didn't feel as though she had forgiven him. He desperately wanted her forgiveness. But the last thing she'd said to him was, "Go away."

Inside the airport, he stood by the glass wall at the arrival area. He held up a sign reading *Miriam Archer* but felt silly. What if he alienated the sister as fast as he had Lisa?

He wasn't sure he could handle it if she looked like Lisa. He hoped Miriam had dark hair and eyes any color but green. He waited, praying for Lisa and hoping that somehow he could avoid offending her sister. *Lord, don't let me say anything stupid.*

She didn't look like Lisa, except for a superficial resemblance. They had the same honey-gold hair, but Miriam's was short and fluffy. Her face was rounder, and her eyes were blue.

She saw the sign as she trudged up from the gate, and headed straight for him.

She was wearing jeans and a maroon parka, and lugging a bulging tote bag. She stopped in front of him.

"I'm Miriam Archer Brown. I think you're here to meet me. Your sign says *Miriam Archer*."

"Oh, yes." He fumbled with the sign, transferring it to his left hand and holding out his right. "I'm Steve Rollins."

"You called me last night, then."

"You're married?" His face went red. "I'm sorry. I just didn't know. On Lisa's ID card, for next of kin, it just said *Miriam*, and your phone number."

"Isn't it unusual for an EMT to meet people at the airport?"

"Well, my sister, Mindy, is Lisa's best friend. Mindy's with Lisa now. She asked me to come."

She smiled then, and Steve caught his breath. Her smile was a carbon copy of Lisa's.

"Thanks so much," Miriam said. "You didn't need to; I could have taken a cab."

"No problem."

"Is Lisa at home?" Miriam's eyebrows contracted so much like Lisa's that Steve stared.

"Uh, yes. She went home this noon, but she's really not up to par. They gave her some Vicodin, and it's really wiped her out. We thought somebody ought to stay with her, so when your plane was held up—" He broke off. "Well, let's not waste time. You have more luggage?"

"One suitcase," said Miriam.

While she waited for the baggage, Steve called Lisa's apartment, and Mindy answered.

"She's still sleeping, but I think that's good. I checked her cupboards, and her sister can find enough stuff for supper."

On the way to the apartment, Steve told Miriam what he knew about the accident.

"So you were actually one of the first on the scene?" she asked.

"Yeah, it was pretty gruesome."

"But she will be all right?"

"That's the official word, but she definitely needs rest. I think the doctor told her to take a week off from work."

"Is that a problem?"

"Mindy says not. She works with Lisa."

"It was such a shock when you called."

"Well, she's had a shock, too. More than one, actually."

"Oh?" Miriam eyed him with apprehension.

"Maybe she should be the one to tell you."

"Is it Bryan?"

"Yes. He's smashed up pretty badly, but…well, apparently Lisa broke up with him. Or he broke up with her; I'm not sure which. But something happened between them last night, before the wreck."

"She said so?"

"Indirectly. His mother called today while I was there, and Lisa asked me to tell her she was no longer seeing Bryan. But she doesn't confide in me. She hardly knows me." He glanced over at Miriam. "Do you know Bryan?"

"I've met him several times."

He wanted to ask her a dozen things. Did she like Bryan? Did she trust him? Had he made Lisa happy? And what could he do to earn her sister's forgiveness?

Miriam chatted pleasantly during the drive, but Steve didn't feel it would be appropriate to lay his heart open to her, and so they discussed the weather and the Red Sox and Clark Media.

When they reached Lisa's apartment, Mindy let them in. He introduced Miriam.

"Lisa still sleeping?" he asked, looking toward the sofa, but it was empty and the afghan was neatly folded.

"No, she got up a little while ago. I helped her into the bathroom, and she's lying on her bed now."

"Well, I'm going to scram. I don't think I'm needed here."

"Thank you so much," Miriam said, taking her suitcase from him.

Mindy smiled ruefully. "Sorry, Steve. She specifically asked me if you'd gone."

"Something tells me she wasn't hoping I was hanging around."

"No, she seemed relieved when I told her you'd left."

CHAPTER SIX

Lisa was very sore on Monday. Her head ached violently, and her ribs were tender from where she'd been flung against the seat belt. Purple bruises adorned her arms, calves, and thighs.

Miriam kept her on schedule for her medication and plied her with soup and juice, without being too smothery. She picked up Lisa's dry cleaning, stocked the cupboards, and caught up Lisa's mending. Lisa was beginning to get a little tired, just from watching her.

"Would you quit it?" Lisa asked at last, from her nest on the sofa.

"Quit what?" Miriam asked in surprise.

"Doing things. Next you'll want to tear the apartment to pieces and spring clean, like Mom used to."

Miriam chuckled, but her color rose a little, and Lisa knew she'd been having that very thought.

"This place isn't dirty, and if you pretend it is, I'll be insulted." Lisa snuggled down under the afghan. "Why don't you get out your cross stitching?"

Miriam shrugged apologetically. "I packed in such a hurry, I forgot to bring it." She sat down in the rocker. "I'm sorry. I didn't mean to make you nervous. I just like to keep my hands busy."

"I know. You always have a project going." Lisa stretched her arms. She was usually active, too, but right now she was exhausted.

"Well, when that Steve fellow called me, I didn't know what shape I'd find you in. I was afraid you were at death's door."

"I'll be fine," Lisa said.

"Your friend, Mindy, said she'd drop by after work."

"That's nice." It was just too hard to keep her eyes open, and Lisa let them droop. She supposed her meds were kicking in. Poor Miriam, she must be bored stiff.

She woke later feeling slightly muddled. Someone was knocking. Miriam brushed past her as she opened her eyes. Lisa winced. Her head was pounding, too. Maybe it was Mindy, although she didn't think it was five o'clock yet. She couldn't remember for certain if they'd had lunch or not. But it didn't matter who it was, so long as it wasn't Steve.

Miriam came to her hesitantly. "Lisa, Mrs. Cooper is here."

Lisa struggled to sit up, blinking. "Sylvia!"

"There, now, you just sit still." Sylvia came toward her, holding out an enormous Boston fern. "I brought you a plant, dear. Thought a little greenery would cheer you up."

"Thank you." Lisa eyed the burgeoning plant dubiously.

"I'll take it," Miriam said. She took the pot from Sylvia and found it a home on the desk as Sylvia shrugged her coat off and held it out toward her. Miriam took it, and Sylvia slid the rocking chair forward so that she sat down just inches from Lisa. "You look terrible, dear. Are you sure you ought to be home so soon?"

"I'm fine. My sister is helping me out."

Sylvia sent a glance of acknowledgment toward Miriam. "Yes, I'm sure it's nice to have your sister here. Is there anything David and I can do for you?"

"No, I don't think so."

"Bryan was awake for a bit this morning, but he's still heavily medicated. We can't get any sense out of him. His father stayed with him while I came over here. We wanted to make sure you're doing all right, dear."

Lisa looked around hazily for Miriam. "Is it time for my pill yet?" Her temples were throbbing now.

"I'll get you some Tylenol." Miriam hurried toward the kitchen, and Lisa wished she hadn't made the request. Now she was alone with Bryan's mother, and she was certain Sylvia would not waste the opportunity.

"Lisa, honey, I came as an ambassador."

"I—I beg your pardon."

"Bryan told us this morning that you'd broken up with him, but he's willing to forgive you if you'll only do one thing for him."

Lisa felt an inexplicable urge to laugh, but managed to hold it in check. "And what would that be?"

Sylvia frowned. "He said you should pick up the bracelet. Do you know what that means?"

Lisa sighed and sank back against the pillows.

"Do you?" Sylvia asked anxiously, bending toward her. "I suppose it's something to do with that stunning charm bracelet he gave you."

Lisa said slowly, "Yes, I know what he means. The bracelet was damaged, and the jeweler is fixing it."

Sylvia's brow cleared. "Well, then it's simple. Tell me where the store is, and I'll go get it for you. Then I'll take you in to the hospital, and you and Bryan can kiss and make up." She smiled so ingenuously that Lisa almost hated to disillusion her. Sylvia Cooper had a rather shallow outlook on life, but she was well meaning, and she had a history of kindness that Lisa couldn't ignore. When Lisa's parents had moved to Florida, the Cooper family had tried to fill the void, and Sylvia had perceived herself as a surrogate mother for Bryan's girlfriend.

"No," she said softly. When she looked up, Sylvia was staring at her in disbelief.

"No?"

"No. I'd rather you didn't get the bracelet. I don't want to see it again."

"But—but honey, don't you want to make up with Bryan? He loves you so! You can't mean this little tiff is a permanent break?"

"That's what I mean, Sylvia." She was very tired. It was too hard to explain, but she could see that Sylvia wasn't satisfied.

Miriam came back with a bottle of spring water and her Tylenol.

"Here, Lisa, take these."

She struggled to sit up and sipped the water, downing the bitter tablets.

Sylvia shifted uneasily and looked up at Miriam, then back at Lisa. "My dear, all couples have disagreements now and then."

Lisa started to shake her head, but put her hand to her temple, pressing her fingers where the pain seared.

"It wasn't an inconsequential spat, Sylvia. I had been thinking for a while that Bryan didn't feel about me the way I'd imagined he did. When I spoke to him about it Saturday, it was obvious that we have different ideas, different ambitions."

"But the accident—"

"We broke up before the accident. I'm sorry it happened, and that Bryan's hurt so badly, but it doesn't change how I feel about our relationship." Lisa shot a pleading glance toward Miriam.

"Mrs. Cooper, Lisa needs to rest," Miriam said gently.

Sylvia looked at her, then back at Lisa. "But—" She sat silent for a moment, then said softly, "I suppose you found out about that girl. That Audra. Bryan sent her away when he woke up, but he told her they would talk later. And then he wouldn't tell us anything about her. But, Lisa, he loves you. There's no doubt about that, child. He wants to patch things up with you."

Lisa closed her eyes briefly, then looked directly into Sylvia's eyes. "I don't want that. I want to be done with it. Right now I'm exhausted, and I'm sore in a thousand places, and I'm sad, too, but I'm not heartbroken. My relationship with Bryan is over, and

I feel free. I think when I've recovered a little, I'll be able to see things clearly, and I'll be glad. I hope Bryan will be, too. Thank you for being so sweet to me, but we'll say good-bye now, Sylvia. I won't be seeing Bryan anymore."

Sylvia frowned and rose slowly. She stood looking down at Lisa for several seconds, her lower lip trembling. Then she stooped and kissed Lisa quickly on the forehead. "Get well," she said. "And good luck."

Miriam stepped forward and held Sylvia's coat for her.

"Thank you for coming by, Mrs. Cooper, and thank you for the lovely plant."

***

Over the weeks that followed, Steve heard bits and pieces about Lisa Archer from Mindy. She was resting at home the first week, and her sister flew back to Nebraska after four days.

Lisa was better and had returned to work. Mindy reported the second Monday. And Bryan was definitely out of the picture.

"Did she ever tell you what happened?" Steve asked Mindy at breakfast one morning late in March.

"Not precisely. It had something to do with the bracelet."

"Don't tell me that."

"It's true. She refused to pick it up from the jeweler. Bryan called her a couple of times, and she told him she didn't want it, or him, in her life anymore."

"So, where is it now?"

"I don't know. Bryan probably went and got it. It was valuable, you know."

"Yes, 18-karat gold."

Mindy raised her eyebrows. "Do you care so much about that bracelet?"

"Not one iota," Steve said. But he cared about Lisa. He knew that.

It had been nearly six weeks, and he couldn't forget her. The way she'd sat on the escalator, so small and uncomplaining while he yanked at the chain on her wrist. The way her eyes had sparked when they'd met at the house. The way she'd folded into his arms when he carried her to the ambulance. The way she'd clutched his hand at the hospital, begging him to check on Bryan. And the way she'd eyed him from beneath her lashes at the apartment. *You're still here*, she'd said with bitterness. *Go away*. No, she hadn't forgiven him.

He could picture her easily, with her luxuriant honey-colored hair and the green eyes that could dance or freeze him like ice. She wasn't small, really. She was taller than Mindy, and slim. Not too thin. She was solid when he carried her, but not heavy. Just a regular girl.

"Maybe he gave it to Audra," Mindy said.

Steve jumped back to the present.

"I wouldn't put it past him to recycle the charms."

"I wonder if he's still seeing that woman," Mindy mused.

"Lisa never had it out with him?"

"I don't think so. I know he's gone back to work. She told me he'd left umpteen messages on her machine, but she wouldn't call him back."

Steve's estimate of Bryan Cooper dropped another notch. If a man really wanted to talk to a woman, there were better ways than stacking up phone messages.

***

Spring was late in coming, and the cold, gray weather matched Lisa's mood. She tried not to let it show, and she was certain she was successful, at least at the office. They'd dealt with some finicky clients, and others had suffered criticism, but she had been praised for her work, for her innovative ideas for graphics. That gave her some satisfaction. Mr. Clark commended her personally for her designs for the Pearson Lumber print ads. But when she was alone, she tended to slip into a brooding melancholy.

It was Bryan's fault, she told herself. He wouldn't let her forget the bitter past. He called her at work one cold morning early in April.

"You had mighty well better retrieve that bracelet, Lisa."

"The bracelet? I told you to pick it up whenever you wanted."

It was true; she had received two postcards from the jewelry store, saying her repaired jewelry was ready. She had ignored them.

"That is your property," Bryan said, and in her mind she saw him gritting his perfect teeth. "It was a gift."

"Then I may do as I choose with it?"

She could hear his angry intake of breath.

"Because I choose to forget about it. If you want it, go get it yourself."

He hung up. She stared mournfully at the receiver, then replaced it. Her property. She had never been concerned about property, but obviously Bryan was. He was having trouble accepting the fact that she was not his property, and was enraged that she had rejected his demand. *Oh, Bryan,* she thought, shaking her head. *Haven't you learned yet? It's not about the bracelet.*

Her phone rang again, and she picked it up warily.

"Lisa Archer."

"Lisa, it's Bob Farmer. Rachel just told me I need to do a complete makeover on the illustrations for the Doherty ads. Can you help me? The client hates the dummies, and I don't know how to fix it."

Lisa sighed. "When does she need it?"

"Today. Now."

Lisa pushed aside the project she had planned to spend the afternoon on. "Bring me what you've got and the concept file."

∗∗∗

Steve stopped at the supermarket on the way home from work. He hated grocery shopping, and usually didn't think much about it. The only problem was, Mindy didn't enjoy it, either, and they'd run out of several essentials. Mindy had insisted that he take a turn to do the shopping, turning a deaf ear when he tried to argue that his schedule was too hectic.

He looked around, orienting himself by the hanging signs. Why was it that milk was always in the farthest corner of the store? Mindy's favorite brand of detergent seemed to be out of stock. She'd berate him if he came home with another brand. Which was better, no detergent or the wrong detergent? He put a small container of another brand in his cart.

It took him several minutes to locate the eggs. They were back in the dairy section, where he'd just come from. That didn't make a lot of sense. Eggs weren't dairy foods. They ought to be in the meat section, next to chicken. He picked out two dozen jumbo brown eggs.

A woman had brought her cart up behind him, and when he turned, he bumped into it and, trying not to lose the top carton of eggs, stumbled and dropped one dozen into the woman's cart. She gasped, turning away from studying the thousand varieties of yogurt, and moved the cart back quickly. That threw him off balance just enough that he reached out for his own wagon to steady himself and dropped the second box of eggs on the floor.

He took a deep breath and stood staring down at the eggs all over the shiny tile floor and his sneakers. Slowly he visually followed the trail of dripping egg whites up to the woman's cart. Several had broken there, smearing her neatly bagged produce, and were sliding in slimy clumps to the floor beneath. She was standing still, staring at him. Steve looked at her hands, clenching the handle of the wagon, and on up to her face.

Lisa. It would be.

I will be nice, he told himself. *I will not say anything sarcastic. I will be the model of humble decorum.*

"Well." She reached for a new package of paper towels in her wagon. The egg flotsam hadn't touched that.

Steve reached toward her. "I'm so sorry. Let me—"

"Don't touch me!"

He flinched. "I'm sorry. I'll clean it up for you."

"No, thanks." She avoided eye contact and tore the plastic wrap from the towels. He wondered if she had recognized him.

"Really, I—"

"Would you leave me alone?" she said. Steve looked around warily, but the other shoppers were ignoring them. Lisa scrubbed at the packages and the metal grid of the cart, catching the worst of the globs of smeared egg yolk.

"Lisa—"

She sighed and looked at him then, pushing back her hair. "This has not been my best day. Things have been strained at work, and my personal life is a shambles. I don't think I can take another confrontation with you."

He nodded cautiously. She knew who he was, all right.

"Look, I—" he began, but she thrust the roll of paper towels into his hands.

"Let's just forget it. Keep the paper towels. Just give the clerk the wrapper and she'll scan it."

He nodded, groping for words that would not offend her.

Too late. She had wheeled her cart and was making a beeline for the checkout. Steve looked down again. No way could he run after her, spreading slippery raw egg all over the aisles.

At least I didn't get mouthy, he told himself. He watched until she turned the corner at the end of the pet food aisle, then stooped to begin the cleanup in earnest. But he knew that later on he'd lie awake, replaying the scene in his mind. In the middle of the night, he would think of ways to stun Lisa with his courtesy. And in his dreams, instead of *Leave me alone,* she would greet him with a heart-stopping smile.

CHAPTER SEVEN

He wanted to call her and apologize. He stared at the phone for minutes at a time, but couldn't quite come up with the right approach.

He could laugh it off. "Hey, sorry about the raw omelet in the grocery store. Maybe we could go out for coffee and scrambled eggs."

No, it would probably be best to play it straight with Lisa. His teasing had gotten him into too much hot water with her already.

But if he spoke truthfully, she'd think he was insane. He couldn't say, "Lisa, I can't forget you. I think about you constantly. I want to spend time with you. I want to know everything about you. I think you're the woman I've waited for all my life." No, she was likely to call the cops if he said something like that.

He and Jimmy had a break between calls late in the evening, and he steeled himself to make the call. He shook free of Jimmy by sending him upstairs in the fire station to look for his jacket. Steve went to the lounge and looked around quickly to make sure none of the other firefighters was within earshot.

Lisa wasn't listed in the phone book, and he mentally applauded her. It was safer that way. He found the number for the office building.

It was disconcerting when Mindy's voice came on the line, but he knew immediately that it was a recording and the company had closed hours ago. "Thank you for calling Clark Media. Our business hours are ..."

He waited until he had the option to ask for an extension according to the employee's last name. His hand shook as he punched in A-R-C for Archer.

"This is Lisa Archer, director of art. I'm away from my desk right now..."

He caught his breath at her cool professionalism. She was all business, yet the inflection of her voice was so singularly hers that it made his pulse race. He could picture her sitting behind a desk, making the recording. She wasn't the type who would agonize over it, she would just do it.

The tone rang in his ear, signaling that he should leave his message. He remembered ruefully the derision he'd felt when he heard that Bryan left Lisa countless messages.

Shaking off the nervousness, he began to talk. "Lisa, this is Steve. Steve Rollins. Listen, I made a mess of things, literally. At the store, I mean. You know, the eggs."

He paused. This wasn't going well at all. He inhaled and said in a rush, "I'm really sorry. I hope you can forgive me, and we can maybe start over. I'd really like to see you again. If you...if you can stand the thought, would you just give me a call?" He left his cell phone number and hung up, feeling terrified and relieved at the same time.

***

The next morning Lisa came into the office dreading the day ahead. She had a week's worth of work to cram into one shift. The light on her desk phone was blinking, and she pushed the button to retrieve messages.

"You have seven messages."

She opened her portfolio and began to unpack it as she listened.

"Lisa, this is Bryan." His voice was belligerent on the tape, and she turned toward the machine. "I've about had it with this thing," he said. "If you don't—"

She hit the erase button savagely, then stared at the machine in dismay. She had erased all seven messages. Oh, well. They were probably all from Bryan, telling her she was irrational.

She grimaced and picked up the receiver. "Mindy, have you got a sec?"

"Sure, what's up?" came Mindy's cheerful voice.

"I had seven messages and I accidentally erased them all," Lisa said plaintively.

"Ooo. Too bad. Can't help you. Oh, the last one might have been Mr. Campbell. He called about five minutes ago, and I transferred him to your voice mail. I don't know about the others."

"Thanks. I'll give Mr. Campbell a call."

***

Three days later, Mindy came to the door of Lisa's office.

"Sorry to interrupt you, Lisa, but there's a package for you."

She looked up, meeting Mindy's eyes. Immediately, Lisa could tell that she had been caught with her guard down. Mindy came toward her quickly and lowered her voice.

"Are you all right?"

"Yes." Lisa crumpled the tissue in her hand and tossed it toward the wastebasket. "Why didn't you take the package?"

"You have to sign for it."

Lisa stood and went to meet the deliveryman in the hallway. He held a small, innocent-looking cardboard box. She frowned. Deliveries to her office were usually files or storyboards, or sample portfolios of artists looking for work. This was much too small. She glanced at the label. Her name and the address at Clark

Media were typed, and the return address was a laboratory across town.

"I don't understand." She stared at the box uncertainly. "I'm not expecting anything from this company."

"Sign here." The deliveryman held out his clipboard.

"I—no." She turned away, to her office.

Mindy followed her in.

"Lisa, what's wrong?"

"I don't like this."

Mindy's bright eyes widened. "What, you think it's a...a bomb or something?"

"No." Lisa sat down hard in her padded chair. "I think it's the bracelet."

Mindy stared at her, then turned to face the deliveryman. He stood in the doorway, holding the package and frowning.

"I've got a schedule, lady. Do you want the package, or not?"

"What if I say not?"

"Then we send it back, *refused.*"

"Do that."

He shrugged.

"No, wait." Mindy came around the desk and grasped Lisa's arm. "If it is from Bryan and you send it back, he'll just find another way to get it to you. You can end this, Lisa. Just take it."

Lisa felt suddenly very tired. She raised her hand to her lips and exhaled slowly. "All right."

The man eagerly brought her the clipboard, and she signed. When he had left with a smiling, "Have a nice day," she sat staring at the box.

"Will you get rid of it, please?"

"What if it's not the bracelet?" Mindy asked. "Don't you think you should open it?"

"No. It couldn't be anything else. Bryan knew someone at the lab, and he got them to put their label on it, so I'd accept it. He knew if it had his address, or the hospital's, or the jeweler's, I'd refuse it."

Mindy frowned. "Well, what if it's something else?"

"You open it." Lisa shoved back her chair. "I'm going for a walk in the park." Sometimes she went there to clear her mind when her work became too stressful.

"If it's not the—"

Lisa took her coat from its hook. "If it's not, you can tell me when I come back. If it is, I don't want to see it, and I don't want to hear any more about it, you understand?"

Mindy nodded bleakly.

Lisa smiled. "Thank you. Just get rid of it for me. Give it away, throw it away, I don't care."

***

Jimmy poked his head into the fire station kitchen, where Steve was starting a new pot of coffee.

"Come on, Steve, we've gotta go over to where your sister works."

Steve turned to stare at him. "What's wrong? Is Mindy hurt?"

"No, they've got a suspicious package."

"That's crazy, Jim. We're not the bomb squad."

"Mindy doesn't think it's a bomb, she just wants to make sure. Her supervisor told her to call someone to come open it. Instead of calling the police, she called our non-emergency line. I answered, and she asked me if you could go over."

Steve sighed. "All right, I'll be back in half an hour."

"I'm going, too. I wouldn't miss this for anything."

"What, me opening a box of office supplies?"

"No, you crossing paths with Lisa again."

"You're too late. We already ran into each other in the grocery store."

"I'm speechless. You didn't tell me."

"It was not my finest moment."

"I take it she put you in your place," Jimmy said with a laugh.

"Again." It still rankled that she hadn't returned his call. At least she could have told him she didn't want to see him.

"Well, Mindy sounded like she thought this was important. Maybe she's determined to make you two be civil to each other."

Steve stopped in his tracks. "You think that's what this is? Some scheme of Mindy's to get me and Lisa together?"

Jimmy shrugged. "All I know is, I want to be there if and when."

***

Steve was all business with Mindy. "What makes you think this package could be dangerous?"

"I didn't say it was dangerous. It's company policy now. If we don't know who it's from, we don't open it."

Steve picked up the small box and read the label. "It's from Fulton Labs, to Lisa Archer."

"Right, but Lisa didn't order anything from them, and she refused to open it."

"Oh."

Jimmy touched his arm. "We'd better take it down in the parking lot and blow it up, Steve."

Steve scowled at him. "With what?" He pulled out his pocketknife and began to slice the tape on the box.

"What if it's—you know—something dangerous?" Mindy's brown eyes were huge.

"Oh, come on. Who would want to hurt Lisa?"

"Where is she, anyway?" Jimmy asked.

"She went out for a while. She should be back soon, if you want to take her statement."

"We're not cops." Steve tugged at the tape with growing irritation. "You should have called 911, Mindy. This is stupid."

"Yeah," Jimmy agreed. "Maybe we should wait. Call the cops and have them come get the box."

"Too late now." Steve opened it and pushed back layers of tissue paper. "Well, what do you know?"

He slid the blade of his knife beneath the chain and lifted the bracelet. Mindy sighed.

"You knew what it was, didn't you?" Steve asked. "You just wasted an hour of city time, Mindy."

"I didn't *know*. Lisa suspected. She told me to get rid of it. I didn't think I should do that unless I was sure what was in it, but I was kind of scared to open it."

"The old doc is persistent, I guess," Jimmy said, leaning on the desk affably, smiling at Mindy.

"Wait a sec." Steve took the bracelet in both hands and spread it out carefully.

"Did the jewelry store fix it?" Mindy asked.

"Yes, that's not a problem. I'd say they even replaced the filigree heart. Right here, see?"

Mindy and Jimmy bent close.

"So what's the problem?" Jimmy asked.

"That charm was number fifteen. Lisa told me that day at the mall."

"So?"

"So, one more has been added, right here, next to the clasp."

Quickly, Mindy counted the tokens. "You're right. Sixteen charms."

Steve nodded. "Bryan must have told the jeweler to add a new one when he sent it for repairs."

"What is it?" Jimmy asked.

"His car. The one we pulled them out of a week later."

Mindy crinkled her nose. "That's weird."

"Why do you suppose he's so insistent she have this thing?" Jimmy asked.

"Ego," Steve said with certainty. "He may have had another woman on the string, but now that Lisa's dumped him, he doesn't want to let go."

Mindy gathered up the tinkling bracelet and lowered it into the tissue paper nest. "Well, she told me if it was the bracelet, to get rid of it. I don't know what to do with it. It's too valuable to just throw away."

"Keep it if you want," Steve said.

"Nah, that's not her style of jewelry," Jimmy said, with a wink at Mindy.

She smiled back at him. "What do you know about it?"

"Not as much as I'd like to."

Mindy laughed, and Steve closed his knife and shoved it into his pocket. "Let's get out of here before I have to start defending my sister."

"Give it to charity," said Jimmy.

"There's a thought. Isn't the fire department having a charity auction next month?" Mindy asked.

Steve nodded. "We do it every year to raise money for equipment that's not in the city budget."

Mindy closed the box and held it out. "Well, here. If you get an appraisal, you ought to be able to raise some change with this. If Lisa ever asks me, I'll tell her it went for a good cause."

Steve took the box reluctantly. "All right. I guess."

Jimmy snatched the box from his hand. "We accept. Thank you very much, Miss Rollins. Are you free for dinner this Friday?"

Mindy laughed. "No, but thank you. Maybe some other time, Jimmy."

"You bet."

Jimmy put the box in the pocket of his jacket and smiled all the way to the elevator. Steve frowned at him as he pushed the button for the ground floor.

"What?" Jimmy asked.

"You."

"Your sister's pretty cute."

"Right." The doors closed, and they rode down in silence.

As they stepped out into the building's lobby, Jimmy said, "So, I'll just take this—"

He stopped, and Steve looked ahead. Lisa Archer was entering the street door. She stopped, too, eyeing them cautiously.

"Hello."

"Hi, Miss Archer," Jimmy said with obvious adoration.

"Lisa," Steve managed. She gave the barest indication of a nod in his direction, but didn't meet his eyes.

There's no way to undo the past, he told himself. *She despises me.*

"How are you feeling?" Jimmy asked.

"Much better, thank you. Thank you both. I never really had a chance to say that after—" She looked toward the elevator, then back at them. "I hope you're not here on business. Is anything wrong?"

"We just popped in to see Mindy," Jimmy said quickly.

Steve was torn between asking if she'd received his phone message and making a cutting remark. He decided discretion was the better part of valor and said, "We need to get back to the station. Good to see you again."

Lisa nodded and moved toward the elevator, but her green eyes were troubled.

Steve looked back just before he went out, but she was already in the car, and the door was closing.

"You were right," Jimmy said genially, heading for the street door. "She hates you."

CHAPTER EIGHT

Steve and Jimmy were helping two of the other firefighters, Jeff and George, wash down one of the ladder trucks. At the main fire station they spent a lot of time cleaning and polishing equipment. It was only the galvanizing calls to action punctuating most shifts that made their job rewarding.

Jimmy sidled up to Steve and nudged him. Steve looked up from where he was scrubbing a tire with a brush and saw her walking across the pavement in front of the station. High-heeled leather boots, short wool coat, and her skirt didn't show beneath it. She was looking around curiously, as though she'd never been there before, but confidently.

He recognized her immediately, but she apparently didn't see him. She approached Jeff, an alluring smile widening as he noticed her and stopped polishing the chrome on the front of the truck.

"Can I help you, ma'am?"

Steve shook his head. Of course she'd go right to Jeff. He was tall and good looking. He'd recently come to Portland from a small town in northern Maine, though, and he was as innocent as a baby. Steve watched with interest as Audra pushed her hair back slowly and sized him up.

"I'm looking for an EMT."

"Sure. Are you injured? We've got two right over there." Jeff nodded toward Jimmy and Steve, never taking his eyes off her face.

Jimmy chuckled and elbowed Steve. "How about that Jeffrey, huh? She's bowling him right over."

Audra smiled and leaned toward Jeff, laying a hand lightly on his wrist. Jeff took a tiny step backward, his back against the fender, and Jimmy stifled a guffaw.

"No, I'm looking for a particular person," Audra said confidentially.

Jeff nodded. He was obviously uncomfortable now. "What's his name?"

"At the hospital they told me it was Steve. I don't know his last name." She held his gaze, and Jeff just stared at her.

Steve decided it was time to put Jeff out of his misery, and stepped out around the truck, where she could see him.

"Excuse me, are you looking for me?"

She turned slowly and eyed him from head to foot. Steve didn't like it, especially with his cuffs all damp from the soapy water, but he was sure Jimmy was enjoying it hugely.

"We met at the hospital," she said.

He shrugged. "I wouldn't say we met, exactly, but I saw you there, yes."

She walked toward him. "You're connected to Bryan Cooper somehow."

He shook his head. "Not really. I was on the ambulance the night of the accident."

She frowned. "But you knew her. The girl, I mean. The one who was in the wreck. She came to his room at the hospital, and then you came looking for her."

Steve hesitated. Freeze her right now, or probe a little? Her eyes narrowed as he watched her, and the image of Lisa's stricken face when she left Bryan's room flashed across his mind.

"Would you like to step inside? We can get some coffee."

She relaxed. "Thank you. That would be nice."

Steve turned and thrust the brush into Jimmy's hands. Jimmy's impish smile was a warning. Steve would have to tell him every single word later.

There was no one in the lounge when they entered, and she sat on the extreme edge of one of the dilapidated green easy chairs, removing her gloves. Steve turned the TV off and poured coffee into his mug and a Styrofoam cup.

"Sugar and milk?"

"No, just black, thanks."

He handed her the cup, trying unobtrusively to get a good look at her ring as she took it. Not a diamond. Amethyst, maybe. He sat down opposite her. "How may I help you?"

She looked down for an instant, then took a deep breath and looked at him with an apologetic smile, but her eyes held determination.

"Bryan never told me there was another woman in his life. That girl—Lisa, her name is."

Steve nodded but said nothing.

"She's stunning."

There was nothing he could say to that without asking for trouble, so he maintained his guarded silence.

"Bryan and I...we were very close."

He sipped his coffee. "How close?"

"We had an understanding, you might say."

He smiled. "There are all kinds of understandings, Miss—?"

"Audra Harrison. It's Ms."

He nodded. Of course it was Ms.

She unbuttoned her coat, revealing a navy tailored suit with an abbreviated skirt, and a lacy camisole peeping out at the neckline. He quickly averted his gaze. She smiled faintly.

"So, Miss Harrison," he said deliberately, "why are you here?"

"Well, I thought maybe you could tell me something about her."

"Why don't you ask Bryan?"

She looked away. "That's fair enough, I suppose." She pressed her lips together, then nodded and looked directly at him. "Bryan and I broke up."

"Recently?"

"After the accident."

"I see."

"Do you?"

"Not totally."

"We were going to be married."

Steve didn't dare respond to that, but he arched his eyebrows in question.

"We were together all through his three years of medical school, and then he began his residency. It was a settled thing."

Steve did some quick calculation. Could Bryan really have known this girl longer than he'd been dating Lisa? Any man would have been crazy to leave Lisa for Audra, as pretty as she was. But to be drawn away from a world-weary woman by Lisa's unassuming beauty, that he could understand. He cleared his throat. "Is it possible that it was settled in your mind, but not his?"

"How long has he been seeing that girl?" Audra demanded.

"This really isn't any of my business. I'm not comfortable discussing it."

She stared at him for a moment. "Fine. I'll ask her. I should have gone to her in the first place."

"No."

She waited, and Steve knew she had him where she wanted him.

"Please don't approach Lisa about this."

"You know her well."

"No, I don't. Really, I don't. But I know she's a very private person, and this would not be kind or wise on your part."

Audra stroked her chin, eyeing him carefully. "So talk to me, Steve," she whispered.

He squirmed a little, but managed to meet her provocative gaze calmly. "That's a beautiful ring."

She glanced at it. "Yes. Bryan said to keep it."

Steve nodded. He probably insisted, the way he had with Lisa's bracelet. "As I understand it, Lisa decided the relationship was at a standstill, and she told him that shortly before the accident."

Audra sat still for a moment, her lips pursed. "So, there was nothing serious between them. Nothing…formal?"

"What do you mean?"

"No…documents?"

Steve frowned. "I don't know what you're asking. They weren't married."

"I meant…" She hesitated, then opened her leather purse. Steve's pulse quickened as she extracted an envelope with two long, scarlet-nailed fingers. She held it out to him, but he didn't reach for it.

"Take it."

"I don't think I want to."

She shrugged. "It's a prenuptial agreement. Bryan owes me $40,000."

CHAPTER NINE

When Lisa pulled into her driveway on Thursday night, she was exhausted. Their presentation to a local real estate company had not gone well that morning. The client wanted all new text for the ad campaign, which had meant changes in the artwork, and she had worked late. She wanted a shower, a bowl of soup, and her bed.

But a strange car sat in her driveway. She pulled up beside it cautiously, unsure whether or not to open the garage door. It was after dark, and she felt suddenly at risk.

The driver's door on the blue car opened, and she pushed the automatic lock button on her armrest. The man approached her car, and her heart pounded. She was about to throw the gearshift into reverse when she realized it was Bryan.

She took a deep breath and lowered her window several inches.

"What are you doing here? You scared me to death."

"Sorry. I just wanted to ask you about—" He stopped and looked down, then leaned against the side of her car, bending closer to the opening. "I'm sorry, Lisa, this is really awkward, I know."

"I told you, I don't want to see you anymore."

"I know. And I respect that. It's just that—well, I find myself in an embarrassing situation, and I wondered if—" He stopped again and sighed.

"If what?"

"No, I can't."

Lisa pushed the button on the garage door opener. "Listen, I'm tired, and I don't want to do this tonight. If you want something, just say it."

"The bracelet."

She stared at him. "I got it. Is that all? It came to the office a few days ago. Are you satisfied?"

"No, actually, I—I was wondering if—well, you said you didn't want it."

"I didn't."

"So, would you be willing to give it back to me?"

She stared at him in disbelief. "Give it back? You're insane. You begged me for two months to take it. I took it."

"And now I need it."

She frowned. "You need it? That's crazy."

"No, trust me, it's not."

"I suppose you want to give it to that other woman." His guilty expression turned her stomach. "Well, forget it, Bryan. I don't have it anymore. I took it like you asked me to, and I disposed of it. It's gone."

"Gone? Where?"

She smiled grimly. "I don't even know. I gave it to a friend and asked her to get rid of it. She didn't tell me what she did with it, and I didn't ask."

***

In early May, Officer Jack Prewitt came to see Steve and Jimmy at the fire station.

Steve had known Jack for some time, encountered him professionally fairly often.

"You boys need to give us some info on an accident that happened February twenty-first." Jack took out his notebook and opened it.

"What accident was that?" Jimmy asked vaguely.

"Lisa Archer and Bryan Cooper," Steve said.

Jack looked at him curiously. "Yes. You know them?"

"Sort of."

"Well, the truck driver, Bernard Smith, was quite convincing with his story, and we're pretty sure from the reports that it was Cooper's fault, but a judge is telling us to reconstruct it. There's a huge insurance settlement and several lawsuits hanging."

"Who's suing?" Jimmy asked.

"Who isn't?"

"Lisa Archer isn't," Steve said with conviction.

Jack raised his eyebrows. "You're right. I was exaggerating. Smith is suing Dr. Cooper, and Dr. Cooper is suing Smith, the manufacturer of the beer truck, the company that made his car, and the city."

Jimmy whistled.

Steve shook his head. "What do you need?"

"Well, you guys moved the car before the cops were done there."

"We had to, to get Miss Archer and Dr. Cooper out," Jimmy said defensively.

"I know, I'm not saying you didn't, but we need to know exactly how things were when you first got there."

Steve rubbed his forehead. "Well, a guy was pulling at the door handle on the driver's side, trying to open it, but it was jammed."

"That would be a witness we've interviewed. Philip Reynolds."

"If you say so." Steve thought hard. "The car was touching the wall of the building on the front end, but Jimmy climbed over the roof and got between the car and the wall."

"That's right," Jimmy agreed. "The front end was buckled, though. We got some cops and bystanders to help us move the whole thing out from the wall, then Steve took Miss Archer out, and then we got the doc out through the passenger side too. He's not suing *us*, is he?"

"Not specifically. Just the city and the ambulance corps."

"Oh, brother," Steve moaned.

"Is this going to involve witnessing in court and all that rot?" Jimmy asked.

"I don't know," Jack told him. "Right now we've got to do the reconstruction and get all the data down. Can you guys come out to the scene tomorrow, about 9 a.m.?"

Jimmy shrugged. "Guess so."

"You should have done this in February," Steve said.

"Yeah, yeah."

***

There was a lighthearted air about the concept meeting for the newest account at Clark Media. Rachel West was in charge of the account, and she was bubbling over with ideas.

"The Red Jacket Restaurant is the proposal capital of Maine, and we're going to make hay with that."

"Sounds good," said Mr. Clark. "Do they want video, or just print ads?"

"Both. Even though this is local, it could be big." Rachel shuffled several papers on the conference table and picked one out. "More men propose to their girlfriends at The Red Jacket than any other restaurant in Portland."

Lisa shifted uneasily. "How can you possibly know that?"

Rachel grinned at her and waved the papers. "Market research. The Red Jacket can document at least fifteen marriage proposals in their establishment in the last twelve months. I called eleven other major restaurants. The closest anyone came is DeMillo's. They said maybe three or four, that they knew about."

"No one else is keeping track," Riley Hunt said with a shrug. He was director of broadcast ads, and was known to be efficient but cynical.

"That's right." Rachel turned toward him eagerly. "A smart hostess at the Red Jacket took notice and started counting, and we're going to use that. She even got the names of the couples, and we might be able to get some testimonials. If we promote the restaurant as the hot spot for marriage proposals, it will be good business all around." There were murmurs of approval, and she went on, "The print ads will be elegant and sensuous—that's your department, Lisa. The video will be upbeat, romantic and enticing."

"You sold me," Riley said.

"Yes, I think this has great potential," Mr. Clark said, smiling at Rachel, and Lisa knew it was settled.

"Great. Lisa, Riley, I want you to have lunch with me at the Red Jacket today."

"Can't," said Riley. "I've got lunch with another client today."

"Tomorrow, then."

He nodded, and she looked expectantly at Lisa.

"Fine," Lisa said. Mr. Clark was pushing his chair back, and Lisa picked up the legal pad she had taken a few notes on. Her doodles included the elaborate chandelier at the Red Jacket as she recalled it. She would definitely include that in the backdrop for the first ad.

She'd been back in her office fifteen minutes before Mindy knocked discreetly and poked her head in.

"Hi," said Lisa.

"I heard about the campaign for the Red Jacket. Are you okay with that?"

She shrugged. "It's only a restaurant."

"Well, I know, but…well, you and Bryan…" Mindy raised her eyebrows and grimaced.

Lisa smiled. "It's not the only place we ever ate."

Mindy stepped farther into the room. "This is pretty nosy, I guess, but is that where he gave you the bracelet?"

"No. No, that was on my folks' front porch, right before he left to go back to med school." Sadness swept over her. So much had changed since then. She smiled up at Mindy. "I'm going to make these ads so great that every girl in Maine will beg her fella to take her to the Red Jacket."

***

"You're not going to bid on that thing." Steve pulled at his collar with one finger, loosening his tie just a bit.

Jimmy shrugged. "Why not? I'm seeing a girl who's into gold jewelry."

"Forget it. You can't afford Lisa's bracelet."

"Well, if the bidding starts low …"

"We want things to go high, remember? Lots of money for the department." Steve looked around at the heaps of donated merchandise to be auctioned that evening. He and Jimmy and a dozen other firefighters had been assigned to help carry items for the auctioneer and take them to the buyers' cars.

"Right." Jimmy shrugged. "All I've got is fifty bucks, anyway. Looks like there are a lot of people in the crowd with fatter wallets than I have."

Steve laughed. "That's good. Come on, time for us to go to work."

It was three hours before he and Jimmy had a chance to communicate beyond a quick word or a wave. Finally the auctioneer lowered his gavel for the last time, and Steve went to help carry a desk out to the parking lot.

When he came back inside, Jimmy called to him. "Hey, Steve, we done good tonight."

"Terrific. Did you see how much the bracelet brought?"

Jimmy winced. "More than I have. You were right about that."

"Who bought it?"

"Some rich guy. Looked like an oil tycoon."

***

Mindy leaned toward the mirror near the coat closet, fiddling interminably with new earrings. This date was special, Steve gathered.

"You're beautiful," he growled, impatient for her to be gone. His sister's social life reminded him that he didn't have one.

"How'd you get tonight off?" Mindy asked. At last satisfied with the earrings, she pulled out a tube of lip gloss and began applying it.

"It just happened. We have a bathroom mirror for that, you know."

It was rare for him to have a Friday night off. He'd let the captain schedule him heavily the past few months.

He looked at Mindy's image in the mirror. She really was cute. Not pretty, exactly, but she had a pleasant face that lit up when she smiled.

"Who you going out with?"

Mindy met his eyes in the mirror. "Are you playing watchdog, or are you just curious as to who would take me out?"

He scowled. Had he been that hard to live with lately?

"I want to know. I don't want you going out with some bum."

She chuckled. "You know Tom Bradley, from church?"

"Tom Bradley? He's married!"

She turned to face him. "Right. But his kid brother's not."

"Oh." Steve picked up an outdoor magazine that had sat on the coffee table for weeks without being read.

"Lisa and I are doubling with Mark Bradley and his friend."

Steve dropped the magazine.

"You and Lisa?"

"Uh-huh." Mindy put her lip gloss in her handbag and pulled out a tube of mascara.

"Lisa Archer?"

"Is there another Lisa?"

Steve sat down on the couch and stared across the room at the blank television screen. When he looked at Mindy again, she was snapping her handbag shut and picking up her car keys.

"Gotta run."

"Hey, wait!"

"What?" She turned back and stood there, poised in her cotton dress and sling-back shoes. Neat and trim, feminine, but not overdressed. His sister was definitely cute.

"I—uh—who set this date up? I mean, is it a blind date?"

"I met Mark last week when he was visiting Tom and Beth, and he called me Wednesday at work. So?"

"Well, what about the other part?"

"What, Lisa's date?"

"Yes."

"You're jealous."

"Am not."

"Yes, you are."

He scowled at her. "Hey, Lisa's got nobody to look after her now."

Mindy shook her head incredulously. "If you must know, Mark asked if I had a friend, you know, a nice, conservative girl. His buddy's kind of blue, and...well, I thought of Lisa. She's blue, too. It's been four months since she and Bryan broke up, and I figure it's time she started going out again. She said yes, so apparently she agrees with me."

Steve couldn't speak. He couldn't look at Mindy, either.

"Oh, Steve, come off it."

"What?"

"This tantrum of yours."

He glared at her. "Lisa went through a lot because of me. I'm just sorry she's been so depressed, all right?"

"Because of you?" She took a step toward him. "That's silly. You know you're not the cause of Lisa's tragedy."

"I'm not? Prove it!"

There was no doubt, Lisa was the cause of his moodiness. He got up and stalked into the kitchen and jerked open a cupboard door. Glasses. He was staring at glasses. He took one to the sink and filled it with water.

"She doesn't blame you for anything." Mindy had come to the doorway.

"She hates me."

"Well, yes, but she doesn't blame you."

He swung around, unable to believe she had said it.

Mindy laughed. "Oh, Steve. You think too highly of yourself. Lisa never gives you a second thought now. Don't tell me you've been brooding all these months, thinking it was your fault she broke up with Bryan."

"Not just that. The accident."

"Oh, now you really *are* omnipotent. And just how did you cause the accident?"

He looked up at the ceiling, then back at her. "It started with the bracelet. We just sort of grated on each other from the first meeting. She was already mad at the doc, I think, but I rubbed her the wrong way. Then she comes here, and I make her even madder. A few hours later she has a fight with Bryan, and he crashes the car."

"She's never told me they fought that night."

"They must have. And if I hadn't made her mad, she might not have torn into him."

"You're speculating."

He sighed. "I saw Doc Cooper last night."

"You did?"

"Yup. At the hospital. We took in a trauma victim, and he was on duty in the ER."

"How does he look?"

"Just the same. You'd never know he was in that accident."

"He probably has residual effects."

"Could be, but you'd never know it by looking at him."

Mindy shook her head. "I wouldn't think a guy like that would need to sue the whole country to support him."

"He's an intern," Steve said uneasily. "They don't make that much." He had his own thoughts on why Bryan had initiated the lawsuit, but he wasn't ready to tell Mindy about that. Even Jimmy didn't know all the details, and he'd kept his mouth shut about the seductive Audra's visit to the main fire station. It seemed best not to burden Mindy with what he knew.

He was angry with Bryan, and he knew he shouldn't be. It was long past time to let go of that. He turned away from Mindy, but she walked slowly over to stand beside him at the sink. She rested her hand lightly on his shoulder.

"This lawsuit has upset you a lot, hasn't it? Look, a judge is going to rule pretty soon that Bryan was at fault, and then it will disappear."

"You never know these days."

"Well, I'm just glad Lisa found out what a chump he is before they tied the knot," Mindy said firmly.

"You and me both."

"Oh, Steve." She put her arms up around his neck, and he reluctantly returned her embrace. "You really care about her, don't you?"

He didn't answer. He couldn't. If he said no, he'd be lying. If he said yes, Mindy would make a fuss, and maybe even tell Lisa he was carrying a torch. They were really close now. Mindy was at Lisa's apartment half the time, even though Lisa never came to their house unless he was at work. He knew that was because she didn't want to see him. At least she hadn't rejected Mindy because of him.

Mindy stepped back and looked at him critically.

"You haven't been out with a girl since the accident, have you?"

He shrugged. "I've been busy."

"Too busy. Well, if it's any consolation, this is Lisa's first date since she and Bryan split."

"She hates me. Why would it console me to know she's seeing another guy?"

"Oh, Stephen!"

"Get out of here," he snapped.

She looked at him pleadingly.

"Sorry," he muttered. "Have a good time."

***

"Well?" Mindy asked coyly as she and Lisa entered the ladies' room at the concert hall. "What do you think?"

"Rick's all right."

"All right? I think he's cute."

Lisa shrugged. "He's nice enough. I'm just not hearing any bells." *Or sirens,* she thought, and immediately squelched that notion. "So how about Mark? Do you like him?"

"Yeah, kind of. He's a little wacky. But I need some frivolity in my life. Steve's a bear lately."

"Really?" Lisa washed her hands too thoroughly, without making eye contact. Her pulse was tripping rapidly, just from hearing his name. It was crazy, but it always had that effect on her.

"It's really silly," Mindy said, pulling a comb from her purse. "He's brooding about the lawsuit from the accident, and he's certain you hate him."

"I don't hate him." Lisa pulled a paper towel from the dispenser.

"He said you took an instant dislike to him the minute you met."

"That's not true." She remembered her ambivalent feelings that day. She hadn't wanted to like him, but she had. And it wasn't just because he was so handsome. She'd been drawn to his competence and assurance, and, yes, as much as she hated to admit it, by his quick wit. "It was just—well, it took me three years to see what Bryan was really like, and Steve saw through him immediately. That made me angry, somehow. I guess what he said crystallized things for me, though."

Mindy said softly, "When you were in the hospital, he apologized for the rotten things he said about you and Bryan. I don't know if you remember; you were pretty doped up."

Lisa opened her purse and rifled it, not sure what she was looking for. Finally she gave up and closed it. Her eyes met

Mindy's in the mirror. "To be honest, I guess there's one thing I've held against him."

Mindy waited expectantly, and Lisa turned away. She couldn't tell Mindy. They were close, but Mindy was close to Steve, too. If she admitted she couldn't forgive him for leaving when she told him to, Steve would know it within hours. And she certainly didn't want him to come back because Mindy told him to.

She didn't want him to know she'd been yearning to see him again, when he obviously had no desire to see her. Even that one time they'd met by the elevator when he'd visited Mindy at the office, he'd left as quickly as possible. If he cared, he wouldn't avoid her so studiously.

No, if he wanted to see her, he'd have done something about it long ago. He was a man of action. He had pulled her from a wrecked car! He had his quota of determination. But he'd walked out of her life and not looked back. Therefore, it was obvious he wanted it that way.

"He didn't mean to offend you." Mindy's eyes were moist as she pled for her brother.

"I'm not offended. It's nothing. It's time I forgot all about it."

"So, you forgive him?"

She hesitated. "Come on, the guys are waiting."

Mindy perked up. "You're going to give Rick a chance?"

Lisa frowned. "His hair's not right somehow."

Mindy's eyebrows rose. "His hair? You'd reject a guy because of his hair?"

"No, that's not what I meant." Lisa leaned on the counter. "Look, Rick's nice, but I just don't think I'm ready for this."

"Honey, it's been months."

"I know." Lisa's voice was small. She didn't want to cry and then have to go out and face Mark and Rick with her face all blotchy.

"You can't mope for the rest of your life because of Bryan."

Not because of Bryan, Lisa's heart screamed. *It's your smart-mouthed brother! If he was just homely, I could forget him. Maybe.* But she knew she'd think about him, even without the gorgeous brown eyes and the fine, thick hair that you wanted to touch to see if it was really as soft as it looked.

Lisa swallowed hard. "I promise I won't mope."

Mindy nodded thoughtfully. "But Rick's not the one?"

"I'll be nice to him, but, please, Mindy, do me a favor."

"You name it."

"Don't set me up with anyone again until I tell you I'm ready."

Mindy frowned, and Lisa could almost read her mind. *What if you're never ready?*

"Some people need a little nudging," Mindy said.

"Tonight wasn't a nudge. It was a shove."

"Okay. I'm sorry."

Lisa leaned over and gave her a quick hug. "Come on, the guys are waiting. We're having fun tonight. I just don't want to get Rick's hopes up. When love strikes, I'll know it, and this isn't it."

Mindy nodded. "Got it."

They went into the auditorium again and down the long aisle toward their seats. They had nearly reached their row when a man in the aisle called her name, and Lisa whirled toward him.

"Miss Archer, isn't it?"

"Oh, hello." Lisa smiled. He was one of her favorite clients, the chief executive officer of a thriving seafood company on the bay. He was in his sixties and gray-haired, but had made it clear at their consultations that he had no plans to retire. He'd loved her illustrations for the ads last fall and the new logo she'd designed for him.

She stepped closer and extended her hand. "Mr. Fossett, this is my friend, Mindy Rollins, who's on the front desk at Clark Media."

"Oh, yes, I thought you looked familiar." Fossett beamed at Mindy.

"Are you enjoying the concert?" Mindy asked.

"Very much." He turned to include the woman at his side. "This is my wife, Cheryl. Sweetheart, these are two of the competent young ladies at Clark, Miss Archer and Miss Rollins."

Lisa smiled and reached toward Mrs. Fossett. "Pleased to meet you."

There was a soft tinkle as they shook hands, and Lisa's attention was drawn to the woman's wrist. She caught her breath and tried not to stare. Her charm bracelet was gleaming softly against the mauve sleeve of Mrs. Fossett's gown.

CHAPTER TEN

Mrs. Fossett followed her gaze and touched the bracelet self-consciously. "I probably shouldn't have worn this to the theater, but I'm fond of it."

"It's lovely," Lisa said, glancing toward Mindy.

Mindy swallowed hard, a blush staining her cheeks.

Mrs. Fossett raised her wrist and turned it slowly. "I adore retro jewelry, and Ted bought me this at an auction a couple of weeks ago."

"I used to have one," Lisa said with a smile.

"Really? My best friend had one in high school, and I always coveted it. I just love the little doggie," Mrs. Fossett said with a laugh. "And here, isn't Cupid sweet?"

"The Porsche is my favorite," Ted Fossett admitted with a chuckle.

"Porsche?" Lisa looked closer.

"My dream car," Fossett confided.

"Why don't you just buy one and get it out of your system?" his wife asked jovially. "You've been driving that Lincoln for two years."

The lights flickered.

"We'd better sit down," Lisa said.

"Yes, our dates will think we ran out on them." Mindy's laugh was a little strained.

"Nice to meet you," Lisa said.

"I'll come see you next month about our fall campaign," Mr. Fossett promised.

Lisa followed Mindy to their seats. "I'm so sorry," Mindy said as soon as they were out of earshot of the Fossetts.

"No problem."

"Hey, I was afraid you got lost," Mark said with a laugh as they rejoined him and Rick.

"No, we ran into one of Lisa's advertising clients. Sorry." Mindy settled in beside him, then leaned toward Lisa. "You sure you're okay?"

"Absolutely."

"See, I gave the bracelet to Jimmy and Steve to put in the firemen's charity auction. I never dreamed you'd see it again."

Lisa nodded. "So that's what they were doing at the office, that day the package arrived."

"Well, yes. You said you didn't want to know anything about it, so I just did what you said and…got rid of it."

"It's fine. The fire department got some money, and now someone who appreciates the bracelet has it." She wondered fleetingly if she ought to tell Bryan she knew who had it now, since he'd wanted it so badly, but decided against that. It was out of her hands.

She did wonder about the sports car charm, but what did it matter? Mr. Fossett had probably bought it for his wife after he purchased the bracelet. Still, it did look like the one Bryan had admired in the jewelry store the day of the escalator incident. She turned her best smile on Rick as the lights dimmed, determined to make their first and last date a pleasant evening.

***

"Look! Steve's in the paper."

Mindy had barged into Lisa's office without so much as a knock, waving the local section of the morning newspaper. It didn't matter, since Lisa was alone and hadn't really started work yet, but for some reason her hackles rose.

Mindy dropped the paper on her desk, and Lisa stared at the photo. Steve Rollins, bending over a stretcher at the scene of a rollover accident. She thought she could make out Jimmy in the background, talking to a police officer.

"Very nice." Lisa pushed it away from her, across the desk toward Mindy.

If her reaction was cool, Mindy didn't seem to notice. She took the paper and went out into the hallway, ambushing any coworkers who happened to walk by, to show them the picture.

As she opened a file and began to work, Lisa battled thoughts of Steve. She'd seen him only twice, briefly, since the day after the accident, and he hadn't been very friendly. But then, neither had she. She remembered her embarrassment in the grocery store, and her need to silence him before he had a chance to push any snide buttons.

But after the accident, he'd been kind. The terror she'd felt just before the crash came back in vivid memory, causing her adrenaline to surge. It seemed like yesterday, although her bruises had long since healed. And Steve. He'd been there within minutes, Mindy had told her later. Was it Steve who had carried her in his arms so tenderly, or was that part of the hazy dreams she'd experienced in her shock and drug-induced sleep?

The newspaper photo wasn't great art, but it had been flattering enough to set her pulse pounding. He looked great in his summer uniform. She knew from Mindy that he worked out three times a week with his friends from the fire station. She looked toward the hallway door, half wishing Mindy would come back in with the paper. She'd only glanced at it. Of course, she could easily buy a copy when she went out for lunch.

No. Absolutely not. It was adolescent to pine over his picture.

And she didn't really need the picture, anyway. All this time, she'd remembered every detail of how Steve looked. What she'd forgotten was how her stomach flipped at the sight of him.

How long is this crush going to last? She'd asked herself that for months now. Adults didn't go on like this, did they? Maybe it would have been easier to forget him if she didn't see Mindy's vibrant brown eyes, so much like Steve's, every day.

That was another thing. Mindy wasn't overbearing about it, but she obviously loved her brother to distraction and was more than a little bit proud of him. She regaled Lisa with the details of his smallest accomplishment, and Lisa always smiled and tried to assume a slightly bored, detached attitude, when inwardly she craved to hear more. She didn't have to work the conversation around to Steve. Mindy talked about him a lot. Not constantly, but enough. Enough to feed Lisa's craving, anyway.

It made Lisa feel terribly guilty, as if she were using Mindy for nefarious purposes. But she genuinely liked Mindy, and had been her friend before she knew Steve existed. Could she help it if her best friend frequently brought up the subject?

She had been careful not to let Mindy in on her guilty secret. Better for Mindy to think there was some dislike there, because the second Mindy figured out that Lisa was attracted to Steve, she would start trying to throw them together. She'd pestered Lisa to visit their church as it was, but Lisa had declined for weeks, then finally forced herself to settle in another one, miles away from the one the Rollins siblings attended. Mindy seemed to get the picture, and respected Lisa's feelings. Or rather, her feelings as Mindy perceived them. Lisa could tell she was disappointed that her brother hadn't "clicked" with Lisa, as she put it. But she seemed to have accepted that now.

Lisa realized she hadn't read a word of the file before her. Who, besides Mindy, was she fooling?

***

In August, Lisa took her vacation and spent two languid weeks in Nebraska with Miriam and her husband. The heat made her edgy.

She sat on the porch with her sister one afternoon, snipping green beans for Miriam to can.

"So, you made a clean break with Bryan," Miriam said.

Lisa snorted. "I thought it was pretty messy myself."

"Did you ever find out who that girl was?"

"I don't want to talk about it."

"But you must have wondered."

Lisa put down her paring knife. "Bryan's mother called me when he left the hospital. It was her last-ditch effort at reconciliation, I guess. She said that Bryan was very contrite, and the other woman was no longer in evidence."

"But you still didn't want to see him again." It wasn't a question.

"Would you?"

Miriam snipped beans rapidly. "Have you met anyone else?"

"Oh, Mindy and I had a double date a couple of months ago."

"And?"

Lisa shrugged. "It was fun, I guess. We went to a concert, then had ice cream."

"Did he call you again?"

"Yes." Three times, she reflected. She had hedged on making another date, and after a while Rick had quit calling. Mindy had been out with Mark several times since, but there were no sparks for Lisa where Rick was concerned, and she couldn't see continuing the relationship.

"There's a guy at our church," Miriam began cautiously. "He's got a farm on the other side of town. He's a widower. No kids."

"Please, Mim." Lisa stood up. "Please, no farmers or teachers or preachers or lawyers. And especially no EMT's."

Miriam looked at her, perplexed, and Lisa walked down the steps and around the corner of the house.

***

"Since when do you loaf around on a Friday night?" Steve asked. He was ready to leave for his shift at the fire station, but Mindy sat listlessly on the couch, with her feet resting on a stack of magazines on the coffee table.

"Oh, Mark's spending the weekend with his parents, and Lisa's on vacation."

"Gone to her sister's didn't you say?"

"Yes."

"Good thing Jimmy didn't hear you're free this weekend. He'd be beating the door down."

Mindy smiled. "He's a lot of fun, but not husband material."

"He's shorter than you, too." Steve glanced at his watch. "I'm heading out. See you tomorrow."

"Steve, wait." Mindy picked up the throw pillow she frequently used as ammunition in their fights over the remote. "I'm worried about Lisa."

"You said she's in Nevada."

"Nebraska."

"Right. So?"

Mindy sighed and picked at the fringe on the pillow. "I didn't tell you, but she saw the bracelet a few weeks ago, that night she went out with Mark and me and his friend."

"What?" Steve took a step toward her, then stopped. "What do you mean, she saw the bracelet?"

Mindy shook her head, wincing. "It was unbelievable. She knows the person who bought it at the auction."

Steve sighed. "Why didn't you tell me this before?"

"I don't know. I guess I feel like it was my fault. I was embarrassed about it, but Lisa said to forget it. She insisted she was glad someone who will enjoy it has it now."

"Who was it?" An awful thought occurred to him. "Tell me it wasn't that Audra woman."

"It wasn't."

"Whew."

"No, it was one of Lisa's clients. He bought it for his wife. They were really sweet, and Lisa didn't tell them it was hers. Mrs. Fossett said her husband took her to the auction and bought it for her. She was very taken with it."

Steve thought about that. "So, what's the problem?"

"Lisa just seems so depressed since then. She'll go places with me, but won't even consider another date. I think that one took the stuffing out of her."

"Because of the bracelet?"

"Partly. And partly because the guy I fixed her up with was kind of dull."

That was somehow gratifying, but Steve tried not to show it.

"Well, that couple got a good deal on the bracelet. It was appraised at two thousand dollars. Some of those charms had real jewels on them. We had quite a few bids on it, but it topped out at twelve hundred."

Mindy nodded thoughtfully. "That's pretty good, I guess."

"Yeah, it was one our best items. All the money from the auction is going toward thermal imaging cameras."

"Still, it's too bad Lisa had to see it again." Mindy sighed and laid the pillow down. "Especially after Bryan came around hounding her to give it back."

"What on earth?"

"Yes. He asked her for it, but I'd already given it to the fire department. Lisa didn't know what I'd done, and she just told him it was gone."

"When did all this happen?"

"She told me that night when we saw it at the concert, but it happened not long after I gave it to you guys."

Steve hesitated. He would be late for work if he got into a long discussion with Mindy, but this was important. He walked over to the couch, and she scooted over so he could sit down beside her.

"Mindy, Bryan is desperate for money."

Her eyes widened. "Why?"

"That woman—Audra Harrison—the redhead—she—"

"Whoa, wait a sec! You know her last name and everything."

Steve nodded. "I didn't tell you before, because I didn't want you to have that knowledge weighing you down when you're with Lisa. Audra came to see me at the fire station last spring. Seems she basically put Bryan through med school, and she's got a legally binding contract that says he has to repay the money."

Mindy sat very still. "How much?"

"Forty grand."

Mindy's breath whooshed out of her. "He was making time with this Audra all through med school? While he was dating Lisa?"

"Yes. Audra claims they were engaged, and the contract was a pre-nup agreement. If they broke up, he had to repay her."

Mindy shook her head slowly. "That's why he kept stringing Audra along, when he wanted to be with Lisa. So he could keep on borrowing money from her and wouldn't have to repay her."

"I don't know. When she came to me, I think it was basically to poke around and find out if he was serious with Lisa. I wasn't going to tell her a thing, but she was thinking of going to Lisa and asking her all sorts of questions."

"She can't go bothering Lisa!"

"Right. So I assured her that Bryan was history as far as Lisa was concerned. But Audra wants her money back, and Bryan's hurting financially now. If the court finds he was at fault in the accident, he'll be hurting even more."

"So he's hoping to make the city pay for it all."

Steve nodded. "Right. It might take him years to pay her off if he doesn't get a settlement." He stood up. "I've really got to go now. Will you be okay? Maybe I shouldn't have told you."

"He couldn't have raised more than a couple of thousand on the bracelet."

He shrugged. "It would be a start. Maybe it would have kept Audra happy for a while. I'll bet she's sued him for the full amount."

"How could he have that fancy car when he was forty thousand dollars in debt?"

"He bought it before he broke up with Audra. I gathered that, as long as she thought he was going to marry her, she didn't want or expect him to repay her. But now it's a different story."

Mindy looked up at him, her dark eyes pleading. "Pray for Lisa, Steve. She's never recovered. I don't mean from the accident. Physically, she's fine. But the emotional trauma has been enormous."

Steve bit his lip. "I do pray for her. Every day."

***

Miriam's husband, Peter, dished out the ice cream, and the three of them sat in the living room with two fans blowing on them.

"You guys need air conditioning," Lisa said.

"We've got other things to save our money for."

Miriam was complacent about it, but Lisa immediately felt guilty. On her salary, she could go out anytime and buy an air conditioner, or anything else she needed. Mim and Peter, on the other hand, had a much smaller income, a monthly house payment, two temperamental vehicles, and a broken clothes dryer. She decided the air conditioner would be her hostess gift to them, to thank them for her quiet vacation.

"What would you like to do tomorrow?" Peter asked. He had Saturday off, and it would be her last full day with them.

"How about we laze around and do nothing?" Lisa said.

"I was thinking we might go horseback riding." Peter looked at her for approval.

"It's so hot," Mim said.

Lisa smiled. "Why don't you take me to see the tree?"

"The tree?" Peter asked blankly.

"Yes, I've heard there is one in Nebraska."

He laughed. "Do I make hick jokes about Maine?"

"No. You're very diplomatic. That's why we allowed you into this family."

"Oh, that was it. Seriously, though, I work with a guy who has horses. He's single, and I thought maybe—"

"No," Lisa said.

Mim grimaced at Peter. "Nothing that smacks of a date."

"Oh. But I thought—" He looked from Mim to Lisa and back.

"I'm not in the market," Lisa said firmly.

"You're seeing someone in Portland?"

"No."

Peter looked at his wife again, but said nothing.

"Lisa's not dating for a while."

He nodded. "I'm sorry, Lisa. I know you went with Bryan for a long time. I just thought maybe—"

"What about that fellow who met me at the airport?" Mim asked suddenly. "You know, your friend's brother. He was very good looking."

"He's overbearing and obnoxious."

Mim blinked. "Really? I thought he was extremely nice."

Peter eyed his wife uneasily. "If we want Lisa to come back and visit us again next August, we need to find some better entertainment than this. There's a place to swim over in Brixton. How about it, Lisa? Would you like to go swimming?"

She shrugged. "Whatever you guys want, but you don't need to entertain me. I love just being here with you."

"Well, it won't be so dull around here next summer," Mim said.

"That's right." Peter smiled conspiratorially at his wife.

"What are you guys talking about?" Lisa asked, sitting up and setting her ice cream bowl aside.

Mim feigned innocence. "Oh, nothing. But you might have to share your room."

Peter's grin was unstoppable. "Someone else is coming."

"A baby," Lisa gasped. "You're having a baby."

Mim laughed. "Yes. I've been dying to tell you."

"Well, why didn't you?"

Mim glanced at Peter. "You seemed so depressed."

"Well, if anything will cure me, this is it. I know what we'll do tomorrow! Let's go shopping!"

"Shopping?" Peter frowned.

"Yes! You'll need a crib and a playpen and—oh, tons of stuff."

"It's a little early for that yet," Mim said.

"No, it's not. Let's drive to Lincoln and make a day of it. We'll take the pickup and fill it. Unless you'd get tired?" She looked anxiously at her slender sister. "When are you due?"

"Not until March. We just found out."

"Well, Aunt Lisa is going to furnish the nursery, and I don't want to hear any quibbling about it."

Peter lifted a hand in protest. "Lisa, that's so sweet and generous, but—"

"No." She stood up. "Don't you dare tell me I can't do this, Peter. I *need* to do this."

"Lisa, sweetie, don't cry." Mim stood up and came quickly to embrace her, and Lisa realized tears were running down her cheeks. "It's all right. We love you so much. And we'll let you buy the crib if you want to."

Lisa swiped at her tears with one hand.

"Are you okay?" Mim asked.

She nodded and sniffed. Peter stood uncertainly, looking to Mim for a cue, and she nodded toward the kitchen. Peter gathered up the bowls and left the room.

"Lisa," Mim said softly, "come sit down. Are you sure you're all right? You've had a rough time the last six months." She reached for a box of tissues.

Lisa took one and wiped her eyes. "Yes. I'm just so happy for you."

Mim smiled. "Thank you. We've wanted this for a while, but, well, you know, money is tight. But we decided we shouldn't wait until everything is perfect."

Lisa nodded. "I think that's wise."

"So, you won't mind sharing your room next summer?"

"Not a bit. I'll even do diapers, with pleasure." She bit her bottom lip, then smiled shakily. "Sometimes I want your life, Mim."

Her sister's eyes widened. "That's silly. Your life is so glamorous."

Lisa laughed. "Oh, right. Don't you realize you have everything I've ever wanted? A husband who loves you dearly, a home together, and now a baby. I'd even live in Nebraska. I want a baby, Mim. Is that awful? I feel guilty just saying it. But I do."

"No, no." Mim pulled her closed to hug her and stroked her hair. "That's normal, and you expected for so long that Bryan would give you all of that."

"I was depending on the wrong person," Lisa admitted. "He's—he's not who I thought he was."

"Then you're better off without him."

Lisa gulped. "I know. I keep telling myself that. But I don't want to be alone forever. I hate it."

Mim nodded. "There's time. Things will get better."

Lisa reached for another tissue. "I know that's true. And who knows? When I get my sanity back, I may even find a man I can trust." She managed a tremulous smile, trying not to think of Steve. She could never trust him with her fragile emotions. Still, he'd been consistent. He'd done what she asked, and now he was out of reach.

She grasped Mim's hand. "And for you and Peter, things are getting better tomorrow. I'm buying you an air conditioner, along with the crib. And we'll call that guy to fix the dryer, too. You're going to need it for all those diapers!"

CHAPTER ELEVEN

Steve was an hour late to work on Monday because of a dental appointment. When he entered the fire station, the ambulance was in its bay. That was a good sign. If Jimmy had been called out before he got there, someone else would have gone with him, and Steve would have found himself putting up with another EMT all day. He was adaptable, but he'd just as soon keep his usual routine and partner. Despite their differences, he and Jimmy got along well.

He looked into the break room and found Jimmy opening cartons of new supplies.

"Hey, Steve, you just missed her!" Jimmy's eyes were bright.

"Missed who? The rookie firefighter?" The men had been talking for days about the newly-hired female firefighter who was to start work that week.

Jimmy frowned. "No, we heard they put her on the late shift. I meant that girl—you know. The one who came to see you before."

Steve stared at him blankly.

Jimmy sighed and reached into the pocket of his uniform shirt. "Audra Harrison. Here's her number."

Steve reached for the scrap of paper reluctantly. "Am I supposed to call her?"

"No, she said she'll come back later."

Steve eyed him critically. "So, what's the phone number for, then?"

Jimmy grinned and snatched it from his fingers. "That's for me."

"You're joking."

"No, why should I? She likes me."

"Jimmy, that woman is poison."

"Nah. She got a bum deal from the doc, but so what? Lisa did, too."

"Trust me, the only thing Lisa Archer and Audra Harrison have in common is an unfortunate past relationship with a certain intern." Steve turned stiffly to his locker. "Did she say what she wanted?"

"Nooo…" Jimmy met his gaze for an instant, then went intently back to unpacking the supplies.

"What?" Steve asked grimly. "Tell me, or you'll wish you had."

Jimmy shrugged. "She did ask me if we'll be testifying about the accident."

"You didn't say anything, did you?"

Jimmy swallowed. "Well, I…It's not a secret that we've been subpoenaed, is it?"

Steve slammed his locker door. "Jimmy, she has a financial interest in this case. She wants Bryan to win a big settlement, so he can pay her off. We, on the other hand, want Bryan to lose, remember?"

Jimmy nodded sheepishly.

"If she comes around here again, you just tell her to buzz off, you understand? And burn that phone number!"

Jimmy wouldn't look at him.

Steve sighed. "You're hopeless. Is this for us?" He picked up a box of bandages, syringes and gauze that Jimmy had set aside for restocking their rig and carried it out to the ambulance bay.

Dread of seeing Audra again and remorse for chewing out Jimmy flooded him as he worked inside the ambulance, and his heart pounded. He fumbled, dropping several packages on the floor. As he stooped to retrieve them, a shadow blocked the light from the rear door, and he knew Jimmy was coming around to settle things.

"Listen, I'm sorry." He looked up into Audra Harrison's face.

She smiled with disconcerting good humor. "Well, I don't know what I did, but it was worth it."

Steve chuckled. "Miss Harrison. I thought you were my partner. He said you'd been here. What can I do for you?" He went to the doorway and down the rear steps.

She smiled up at him, tilting her head to one side. The gray-blue eye shadow on her eyelids glittered a little. Steve looked away. Lisa or Mindy would never plaster on the makeup like that in the daytime. If she was pretty, it was in an artificial, slightly ridiculous way. He supposed Jimmy found her artistically-applied embellishments attractive.

"Steve," she all but purred, "could I have a word with you?"

At least the dread was over. Now he was just plain uncomfortable.

"Miss Harrison, if this is about the lawsuit, then the answer is no."

Her eyes narrowed, and her crimson lips formed a perfect pout. "Call me Audra. I'm only trying to find out if I have any hope of recouping my losses. Surely you can understand that."

"Well, you're asking the wrong person."

"But you and Jimmy Bickford will be testifying. He told me so."

Steve shrugged. "It's part of the job. I can't tell you anything."

"But you must know how it's going to go. It's important to me, Steve." Her long white fingers touched his sleeve, but he didn't feel any warmth. "I've had a rough time of it since Bryan and I split up. I've got my job, but I was counting on—on my fiancé for security. Now I don't have that. I need to know what to expect." Her fingers stroked his wrist slowly.

Steve stepped back. "We shouldn't be having this conversation, Miss Harrison."

"But we are."

"Well, it's over." He nodded and stepped toward the hallway that led to the offices and the lounge. Jimmy stood in the doorway.

"Here, Steve, some more saline for the rig."

Steve looked at the box, but didn't take it. "Excuse me, Jimmy. You take care of it, please." He walked past him, down the hall and into the kitchen. He poured himself a cup of coffee and took a big swallow before a stab of pain reminded him that the dentist had said his teeth would be sensitive for a few hours.

A bell began to ring, and the dispatcher gave the orders over the speaker. Steve hurried back to the bay. Audra was standing very close to Jimmy beside the ambulance. She was several inches taller than him, and Jimmy was laughing up at her. Steve grabbed the box from Jimmy's hands.

"Come on, we've got to roll. Miss Harrison, you'll have to leave now."

***

When Lisa stepped off the elevator at Clark Media, Mindy jumped up to hug her.

"I'm so glad you're back! How was your vacation? Did you have a good time?"

She walked down the hallway with her, toward Lisa's office, eagerly recounting all the office happenings of the past two weeks.

"I heard Bob Farmer is going to retire at the end of the year."

Lisa smiled. "So, there might be an opening in the art department."

"Could be."

"You're number one on my list of applicants. I'll let you know the minute I hear anything."

"Thanks. Oh, Mr. Fossett was here Thursday for a meeting with Al Decker on his fall campaign. And it looks like we'll be handling Hobart Auto's advertising now."

"Really? That should be a big account."

Mindy paused outside Lisa's office door. "You'll never guess what I did Saturday."

"What?"

"Oh, come on, guess."

"Went skydiving."

"No, I went deep sea fishing with Jimmy Bickford."

Lisa was stunned. "What happened to Mark?"

"He's still in the picture, but we're not to the serious stage, and besides, he's going back to grad school. Won't be here again until Thanksgiving."

"Well. Did you have fun?"

"A riot. Jimmy is so funny! We're going to the fair in a couple of weeks. Come with us, Lisa."

"With you and Jimmy? I don't think so."

"No, with me and Jimmy and Steve."

"In that case, absolutely not."

"Oh, come on," Mindy coaxed. "It wouldn't be a date. Just friends, the four of us."

"No. I hardly know Jimmy and Steve. Besides, Steve and I never got along." Lisa opened the door and entered her office, laying her portfolio on a chair near the coat hooks.

Mindy followed her. "I thought you forgave him a long time ago."

"Forgiving someone and going out with him are two different things."

Mindy sighed. "It would be so much fun."

"For you and Jimmy, maybe. For the rest of us, it would just be awkward. You haven't already asked Steve about this, have you?"

"Well, not yet."

"Don't. He would hate the idea."

"How do you know?"

"Please, Mindy. Let's not."

Mindy turned toward the hallway, her shoulders drooping. Lisa picked up her portfolio, ready to get down to business.

"Mindy!" She startled herself, her voice was so loud and shrill.

Mindy was at her side instantly. "What? What's wrong?"

"What is that thing doing on my desk?"

Mindy gasped. "I don't know."

Lisa stared at the bracelet that lay on a thick file folder, fanned out in a perfect sunburst.

***

"It's the ideal nostalgia campaign," Al Decker insisted. "Mr. Fossett had the basic idea, and Ed and I fleshed it out. I thought it was kind of weird at first, but it grows on you."

"I don't like it."

"You don't have to." Decker leaned back in his chair. "All you have to do is make the storyboards and sketch the charms."

Lisa shook her head helplessly. "What does a charm bracelet have to do with clam chowder and crab legs?"

"It's an old family company. Family, memories. Memories, heirlooms. Get it? We film the bracelet, then zoom in on one of the charms, say the sailboat. Your sketch of the boat dissolves into a live-action shot of a family sailing."

"And eating clam chowder?"

"Something like that. The next ad features the family dog. This guy right here." He held up the bracelet, taking the dog charm between his thumb and index finger.

"I've seen it. I still don't like it."

"What's not to like? The dog charms fades and the real dog comes up, playing with Dad and the kids. Mom calls them in for oyster stew. The next ad is the stethoscope. A doctor eating Fossett's shrimp for lunch."

"It's awful."

"Mrs. Fossett loves it. Ergo, Mr. Fossett loves it."

"So we have to love it?"

Decker shrugged. "I think you're smart enough to make it work, Lisa."

She drew a slow, deep breath, casting about for a way to convince him that the concept wouldn't work.

"Mr. Clark has already okayed it," Decker said. "Our next meeting with Mr. Fossett is a week from today. I want sketches of the first six charms ready by then."

***

"Stop over there," Jimmy said, pointing to a parking spot.

"What, in front of the flower shop?"

"Yeah. What kind of flowers does your sister like?"

"You're sending Mindy flowers?"

"That's right. We had fun Saturday."

"Are you seeing her again?"

"Hope so. Flowers ought to clinch it."

Steve parked the ambulance. "Hurry up. This time will have to come out of our lunch hour. I'll call it in."

He waited impatiently for ten minutes, until Jimmy climbed back into the ambulance cab.

"My credit card's smoking," Jimmy laughed.

"What did you send her?"

"Fall flowers in a coffee mug for Mindy, and a basket of piney-looking stuff and carnations for Heather."

"Heather?"

"The new girl in dispatch. I asked her out for Thursday."

Steve sat staring at him. "And where does Audra fit in?"

"She doesn't. You're right. She was just fishing for information."

Steve shook his head. "Well, I'm glad you saw through that."

"Like a tripled-glazed window."

Steve laughed. "You must be referring to her makeup job. But still, you sent flowers to two girls on the same day."

"Just covering all my bases."

"I just helped you two-time my baby sister."

Jimmy scowled at him. "What are you talking about? I'm not going steady with either of them. I just like to do things the classy way."

Steve started the engine and pulled out onto Congress Street. "Now I know why you're always borrowing money from me."

"Mindy had fun Saturday, didn't she? After she got over being seasick, I mean."

"Yeah, she said she did."

"There you go."

Steve sighed. "Don't you ever want to settle down, Jimmy? Come home to the same woman every night?"

Jimmy blinked at him. A glint of mischief lit his eyes, and he said playfully, "You do that now. How is it?"

***

"I hate this campaign," Lisa said. She kept her voice low, but couldn't keep the passion from it.

"I'm sorry." Mindy laid a magazine and two folders on her desk. "Too bad you were away when Mr. Fossett came in with the concept. He asked for you, and seemed disappointed that you were away. You might have been able to steer him toward something else."

"I'd actually been thinking some about his ads while I was in Nebraska. But now we're stuck with this." She nodded toward the spurned bracelet, lying in a compact heap on her desk.

"Is there anything else you need from the library?"

Lisa sighed and stretched. "No, but I could use a cup of tea."

"Sure."

"Wait, better make it coffee. I'll be here late again tonight."

"I guess it's too late to come up with another idea."

"Much too late. Al Decker is committed to it, and he's already got Mr. Clark's approval."

"So, nothing you suggested would matter."

Lisa frowned. "Well, it would have to be a stupendous idea."

Mindy left the room, and she picked up the bracelet. Might as well use the snowman charm for the fifth ad. It would have more longevity than the Christmas tree. Maybe the concept wasn't as awful as she'd thought.

She stared at the filigree heart. It didn't remind her of the giver. Instead, it pulled her thoughts back to the day he'd bought it for her. The day she'd met Steve.

How was it that every time she looked at the bracelet Bryan had bought her, she thought of another man? It didn't make sense.

She threw the bracelet down on her drawing board and went to stand at the window. At the crown of the huge maple outside was a cluster of broad green leaves edged in crimson. Last year at this time she had been waiting eagerly to hear from Clark Media, hoping ardently to land a job here. A job she would never grow tired of, because she loved turning ideas into visual art. She loved hearing the client say, "Yes, that's exactly what I want." At the moment, it didn't seem to have turned out the way she'd envisioned it.

She would take a break from the Fossett's campaign and go over the proofs for Hobart's Auto. That would refresh her mind for another session with the hated bracelet. Why, oh why, did Mr. Fossett have to go to that auction, anyway?

Her phone rang, and she picked up the receiver.

"There's a Raymond Berger here to see you," said Mindy.

"Never heard of him."

"He has a briefcase."

"Not a portfolio?" Sometimes artists looking for work waylaid her.

"Definitely a briefcase," Mindy said softly.

"All right. Forget the coffee for now."

Mindy showed him in, and he was to the point.

"Miss Archer, I'm Ray Berger, with Berger, Tine, and Carson. We represent Dr. Bryan Cooper in a civil lawsuit."

Lisa was wary. "What does that have to do with me?"

"You're a potential witness for us, Miss Archer. You were in the car with Dr. Cooper the night of his accident. We'd like to get a deposition."

"What makes you think I'd be a friendly witness for Bryan?"

"Surely personality clashes wouldn't affect your testimony." Berger smiled knowingly, and she wondered what Bryan had told him.

"I was injured, too," Lisa said.

"Yes," Berger said thoughtfully. "I suggested to Dr. Cooper that you might want to join the suit."

She laughed shortly. "No, thank you. If I were going to sue anyone, it wouldn't be that truck driver."

"Oh?" Berger's brows shot up. "Dr. Cooper assured me you'd be sympathetic to his case."

"Dr. Cooper was wrong."

"Well, we ought to sit down and discuss it, hear your account. The police report was sketchy. They never interviewed you after the accident?"

"I was unconscious. That would make it difficult."

"But surely, later—"

"An officer phoned me when they were reconstructing the accident, that's all."

"Hmm. Well, I really think we need to get your statement on tape, Miss Archer."

Lisa's mind whirled as she tried to follow each possible course of action through to its probable result. She looked Berger in the eye. "Please leave."

"I beg your pardon."

"You heard me. I don't want to discuss this."

"Please, Miss Archer, if you take it that way, we'll have to get a court order."

"I'm sure you can get one."

He drew a deep breath. "Really, Miss Archer, let's not make this more difficult than it has to be. I'm sure you don't want to cause extra problems for Dr. Cooper."

"Why wouldn't I?" She met his stare coldly.

Berger picked up his briefcase. "If that's the way you want it."

She went back to the window and stood staring at the tree for several minutes. She needed some advice, and fast, but she had no one to call. Her bosses knew art, not law. The firm did have a legal consultant, Rodney Greer, but she hesitated to call on him. He had a way of trying to turn every conversation into a flirtation. He had asked her to lunch several times, and she had held him off, declining graciously, but she knew he still had his eye on her. Every time he came to the building, she hid in her office to avoid being ogled.

But she couldn't think of anyone else to ask.

"Mindy, could you please get Mr. Greer on the phone for me?" she said into her receiver.

A minute later the phone buzzed.

"Lisa, Rod Greer. What can I do for you?"

"I have a legal question, Mr. Greer. Would it be possible for us to discuss it today?"

"By all means. One o'clock at the Last Dodo?"

Lisa grimaced. The trendy restaurant was not her idea of the place for a business lunch.

"How about Nelson's Family Restaurant?"

"Oh, well, if you prefer. I'd be delighted to meet you anywhere."

"It's business, Mr. Greer."

"So you said. And it's Rod."

***

"You're having lunch with Rod Greer?" Mindy was incredulous. "But, Lisa, he's got an awful reputation."

"I know." Lisa sighed, leaning her chin on her elbow. "I didn't know who else to call."

"Does this have anything to do with the man with the briefcase?"

"Yes. He's Bryan's lawyer. They want me to testify to something that will make a court give Bryan heaps of money for cutting out in front of that beer truck."

"Yikes."

"Right," Lisa agreed. "I won't lie, and I don't want to get within five miles of Bryan, or – or have to testify. Period."

Mindy touch her hand. "I'm sorry you have to go through all this. You were just starting to get over it."

Lisa's glance fell on the gold bracelet that she had left lying on the drawing board. "It's been harder than I thought it would be, Mindy."

She had begun to let go of the whole mess. But if she had to relive it all now, the churning emotions would come back, keeping her awake at night, depressing her all day. And she would be forced to come face to face with Bryan at the courthouse. Well, she thought she could handle that if it was absolutely necessary. But what about the other witnesses? Would the police officers and EMT's who responded to the scene be called? If Steve and Jimmy were there, too…She really didn't want to face that.

She looked at her appointment book. "Just call Ms. Langston and ask if we can reschedule our meeting for tomorrow, all right?"

"Sure." Mindy turned toward the door, then looked back. "Lisa, I had a thought," she said timidly.

Lisa smiled. "I'm sure you've had lots of thoughts, Mindy. What in particular?"

"Well, it may not be anything, but I was thinking about how Mr. Fossett likes the family tie-in for the ad campaign."

"Right. His great-grandfather started the company a hundred years ago."

"Well, I was thinking …"

"What?" Lisa's curiosity was piqued now.

Mindy pulled a small pewter frame from the pocket of her jacket. "See this picture?"

Lisa turned it toward her and smiled involuntarily. "You and Steve?"

"Yes."

The children were muffled in puffy snowsuits, standing proudly in front of a snow fort.

Mindy eyed her cautiously. "Family pictures make people all fuzzy and happy inside."

"And?"

"Suppose that picture was of Mr. Fossett's children. He does have children, doesn't he?"

"I don't know—yes. He mentioned once that his son is in the company."

"Well, maybe they have some cute pictures of the children. Or of the grandpa who founded the business. You know, old black and white—"

"Yes!" Lisa saw it suddenly, full blown in her mind. "Grandpa Fossett, the family patriarch, holding up a fish he caught. Dissolve to today's company president holding the product."

Mindy smiled. "It was just an idea."

"This could be what we need, Mindy! It will make it more personal." She grabbed her purse and sweater and walked down the hallway with Mindy as she talked. "I've got to get over to the restaurant to meet Rod Greer. Pull everything on the company's history for me. And can you call Mr. Fossett and ask for a consult? I'll meet him anywhere." She paused at the elevator door and turned quickly. "On second thought, ask him if I can visit him and Mrs. Fossett at home."

"At home? Are you sure?"

"Yes. Where their photo albums are. Mrs. Fossett is very sentimental, and I have a feeling she won't mind showing me their photos. If Mrs. Fossett likes the idea, her husband will like it."

Mindy nodded, her smile growing as she considered Lisa's suggestion. "But what about Al Decker?"

"If the client likes it, Al will like it."

The elevator door opened.

"I'll make sure you get some credit, too." Lisa stepped into the car.

"Pick up a gift for Mrs. Fossett," Mindy called as the door closed. "A bone china teacup, maybe."

***

"So why aren't you on the city's witness list?" Greer asked, sipping his wine.

Lisa had insisted they skip the small talk, turning his compliments aside. She was all business, frosty and efficient. She wanted to know her rights.

"I don't know. Maybe they think I'd be hostile. Do I have to testify?"

"Not unless they subpoena you," Greer told her, "but if you really want to see justice done, you might want to go forward and offer your services to the opposition. I mean, if it happened the way you say, Cooper shouldn't be rewarded. And your testimony ought to be the clincher."

"I was hoping to avoid appearing in court."

"Well, the truck driver's counsel should have contacted you long ago. Sloppy work, if you ask me. If you really want to keep this guy from collecting—well, I'd go see the trucker's attorney if I were you."

She sighed.

"You'll be the most beautiful witness in court." His smile was almost a leer.

Lisa scowled. "Please, this is business."

"I'm not charging you a fee for this advice. Therefore, it's not business. It's social."

"Send me a bill," Lisa said. "Thanks for the advice. This is for my part of lunch." She tossed a ten-dollar bill on the table and walked away.

***

Steve dragged himself out of bed the next morning, so he could see Mindy before she left for work. He hardly saw her anymore. These double shifts were getting to be too much What good was the overtime pay when you never had time to enjoy it?

Mindy was eating cereal at the kitchen table, which was brightened by a small gold and orange floral arrangement.

"Look what Jimmy sent me! Isn't that sweet?"

"Sweet." Steve went to the cupboard for a bowl.

"I like Jimmy a lot, but I'm not sure what his shelf life would be. Do you think he's serious?"

"Jimmy's never serious." Steve took the Wheaties back to the table with him. "Are you going out with him again?"

"Maybe. I think so."

"Hm."

"What does that mean?"

Steve shrugged and poured his cereal. "Don't get your heart broken."

"By Jimmy?" Mindy laughed. "I think of him as safe. We can have fun together, no pain in sight."

"Do what you want."

She sobered. "Don't you trust him?"

"Well, I don't know. I trust you, though."

She smiled. "Thanks."

"Wear the blue dress."

"Huh?"

"The blue dress you wore to Gail Turner's wedding. It's a killer dress. But wear flats."

"Excuse me? He was talking about going to the fair. I'm not going on the Tilt-a-Whirl in a dress."

"Right. With Jimmy, better wear jeans and a sweatshirt."

Mindy's soft brown eyes shone with tears. "You think I look okay in that dress?"

Steve shifted uncomfortably. "How do I know? I'm your brother."

"I don't have Mom around to boost my self-esteem anymore."

He poured the milk carefully and set the pitcher down. He hadn't thought much about how Mindy was affected when their parents moved to Florida. They saw them a couple of times a year now. He missed his mom and dad, but it was just part of growing up. Mindy seemed to be taking it harder. Maybe girls needed more support from their families.

"Okay," he conceded. "You look terrific in that dress. And I'm not just saying that. It's your color. Or something."

"Thanks, Steve."

"You're welcome."

"Hey, would you consider a double date?"

"With you and Jimmy and who?"

"Oh, I don't know."

"I don't think so."

"Even with L—"

"Don't say it."

"Oh, come on."

"You know she hates me."

Mindy sighed.

"But I gotta tell you—Jimmy dates a lot of girls."

She laughed. "I know."

"No, really. He's seeing someone else tomorrow night. I don't want you to think you're the only woman he has eyes for."

Mindy reached over and squeezed his hand. "Thanks, but I told you, it's not serious. I'll save the dress for someone else."

CHAPTER TWELVE

The case came to court after Thanksgiving. Across the city, Christmas displays were shouting *Peace on Earth*, but Steve felt anything but peaceful. He was restless and dissatisfied, although he had deeply buried his longing for Lisa. He pushed himself relentlessly at work, taking extra shifts whenever he was asked. Mindy moved in a different sphere, crossing paths with him occasionally at the breakfast table. He dreaded the hearing, but accepted it as inevitable.

On the appointed day, he and Jimmy went to the courthouse and sat on a bench in the hallway, waiting to be called into the courtroom.

"I can't believe it's gone this far," Jimmy said. "The judge should have thrown it out." He slumped back against the wall.

"I'll be glad when it's over," Steve said. He knew Bryan Cooper was in the courtroom, and Bernard Smith, the injured truck driver, had been called in ten minutes earlier. Any time now, the bailiff would come for them. He would be technical and efficient, but emotionless when he gave his testimony, and then he would leave and forget it.

"How's Mindy?" Jimmy asked.

"She's all right. You two aren't seeing each other anymore?"

Jimmy leaned back with a smile. "Mindy's a great kid, but…I don't think we'll ever be more than good friends. That's not to say I'd never go out with her again, but, you know, it would be for fun."

Steve nodded. "No offense, but I'm glad." Mindy deserved a man who would cherish her, and he couldn't see Jimmy in that role. But Steve wanted that for her, even if he never had it in his own life.

"Hey, lookee!" Jimmy was at attention. Steve turned and looked down the hallway.

Lisa Archer had entered the building and was walking slowly toward them, studying the legend on each door she passed.

Jimmy jumped up and went quickly toward her. Steve stood slowly, unable to turn away or go forward.

"Miss Archer!" Jimmy cried with genuine delight.

She looked up, startled, then smiled. "Oh. Mr.—uh—Bickford, isn't it?"

"Jimmy Bickford. Hey, you look great."

She flushed and grasped his hand for a moment. "Thank you. I thought I might see you here. I want you to know, I think this lawsuit is terrible. You and—and your crew were terrific that night. The city shouldn't have to defend itself."

"No big deal."

"Yes, it is," she said sincerely, slipping off her wool coat.

Steve drank in the sight of her. The suit was perfect. Soft lines, but professional, in a deep, conservative green. He couldn't see her eyes from where he stood, but he knew they would glint a lighter green. She looked thinner, and she wore no jewelry, except a pendant watch on a silver chain around her neck.

She saw him then, and their gazes locked for an instant. He couldn't just stand there staring. He stepped forward numbly.

Jimmy half turned toward him. "You remember my partner, Steve, don't you?"

"Certainly." Her smile was perfunctory.

"Lisa." His voice was thick. "How are you?"

"I'm well, thank you." She didn't meet his eyes, but looked around expectantly. "So, I guess I'm in the right place for the hearing."

"Yes." Steve couldn't stop looking at her. The old yearning broke loose and filled his heart, making his breath a little ragged. He cast about for a topic, any topic, that would keep her there beside him. "We're supposed to wait out here." With a jolt, he realized she was looking at him now, and holding his look. It was almost as if she were touching him. *You're nuts,* he told himself.

Jimmy cleared his throat and said brightly, "Well, I'm gonna get some coffee. You two want some?"

"No, thanks," Lisa murmured, still watching Steve's face.

"No," Steve said. Jimmy sauntered away. "Hey, would you like to sit down? Someone's going to come tell us when they need us."

She sat on the bench with her back straight against the wall, her coat clasped with both hands on her lap.

"May I hang that up for you?" Steve reached for the coat, and she let him take it. He walked quickly to a coat rack and hung her coat next to his, then took a deep breath and turned back to the bench, his nerves playing havoc with his reasoning. He sat down beside her, careful to keep a slight distance between them, but not so much as to seem unfriendly, and found himself grappling with possible opening lines.

"I'm sorry you were dragged into this," she said, and he sighed with relief.

"It should be over soon." It was almost worth all the bother, he thought, to see her again. He eyed her cautiously. "How are things going at work?"

She blinked rapidly, then looked at him. "It's hectic, but all in all, pretty well."

"Mindy told me about Fossett's Seafood." Immediately he regretted mentioning the Fossett's account. He didn't want to remind her of the ill-fated charm bracelet.

Her smile was a little shaky. "Mindy got me out of a very difficult situation on that one. Did she tell you? She had a fantastic idea for the ads."

"She told me. She was pretty excited about it."

Lisa's expression had softened. "She's very talented."

Steve nodded. "I always knew it, but she didn't think she'd get very far without her degree. She said you put her name in for the promotion. Thank you."

"She deserves it. It's going to be great having her in my department after New Year's." She looked down the bleak hallway and pulled in a sharp breath.

"Are you nervous?" he asked.

She swallowed, then looked at him. "Very. I've been trying to forget the accident and everything that happened afterward. Now I have to bring it all up again." She ran the strap of her purse fretfully through her fingers.

"Do you even remember that night? You were pretty shook up."

"The part after the crash is pretty blurry, but …" She bit her upper lip and glanced at him. "I remember the part before. It's very clear."

Steve nodded soberly. "Well, that's all the judge needs to hear, I guess."

They sat in silence for a moment, then she asked softly, "How about you? Are you nervous?"

"Not really. I've had to do this quite a few times." *Funny,* he thought, *seeing you is more nerve-wracking than testifying in court.*

"Mindy said—" she stopped and looked down at her hands, and her color deepened.

"What?"

"Well, I know you go to church together every week."

"Yes."

"Do you pray?"

He watched her intently for a moment, wondering where that question had come from, before he said softly, "Yes."

"Would you—would you pray for me when it's time …" She searched his face, then looked away.

"Of course."

She smiled then, an anguished smile. "Thank you. I know I shouldn't let this get to me, but I've never really told anyone about what happened that night, not all the details, anyway. And now I have to do it in public, and I'm afraid Bryan will be in there and—" She stopped suddenly and took a jagged breath. "I'm sorry."

"It's all right." He reached over and touched her hand gently. "You'll be fine."

She grasped his fingers and turned to face him. It was unexpected, and he almost pulled away, but sat still, meeting her intent gaze, a surge of warmth rushing from his hand to his heart.

He was sure it couldn't mean to her what it meant to him. He remembered that night at the hospital, when she had held his hand. Maybe it was like that moment, when she'd had no one else to comfort her, and she had reached out to him in desperation.

He wished the sweet torture would continue forever, but the door to the courtroom opened and the bailiff came into the hallway.

"Lisa Archer," the man intoned.

Lisa stood, and Steve got up, too.

"May—may Mr. Rollins and Mr. Bickford come in now, too?" Lisa asked. Steve saw that she was shaking.

"It's not the usual procedure," the bailiff said.

She took a deep breath. Steve thought she looked like a damsel facing the guillotine.

"Is there any law against it?" he asked.

"You'll be called when it's time," the bailiff replied.

Steve squeezed her hand gently, then let go of it. She swallowed hard and stepped away from him. The door closed behind her and the bailiff.

Steve stood there breathing carefully, wondering how long he would be able to smell her fragrance. He sent up a silent prayer, in answer to her plea.

Jimmy strolled back carrying a Styrofoam cup of coffee.

"I told you last spring to send flowers," he said regretfully.

Steve sat down hard on the bench.

"When do I listen to you?"

"You should." Jimmy sipped the coffee. "Gorgeous girl. If I weren't your best buddy, I'd try to charm her myself."

"Please," Steve said with dignity, "don't use the word *charm* in reference to Lisa Archer."

***

"Rollins, Bickford, you can go now." The bailiff stood in the courtroom doorway.

"We can go in?" Jimmy asked, jumping up off the bench.

"No, you can leave. The judge says we don't need you."

"We've been here two hours," Steve protested.

The man shrugged. "That's life." He went inside and closed the door.

"Come on," said Jimmy. "Let's go back to the fire station."

"Don't you want to hear what the ruling is?" Steve was annoyed. It wasn't that he had wasted his time. Seeing Lisa for five minutes out of a hundred and twenty was not a waste of time. But he realized he'd been anticipating seeing her again, if only for another five.

He wanted to know that his prayers had been answered, that God had given her the courage and stamina he had asked for. And he wanted to know that Bryan Cooper was not getting taxpayer money when he had caused the accident.

"It might be hours before they come out of there," said Jimmy. "Let's go."

Steve retrieved his jacket, and he and Jimmy walked down the long hallway. The front door opened as they approached it, and Audra Harrison came in, squinting in the dimness.

"Well, hello," Jimmy said with a grin.

She blinked at him. "Oh, hi, Jimmy. And Steve!" Her eyes widened as she smiled at him, and Steve nodded curtly.

"Is the hearing over?" She looked at him intently, then back at Jimmy, as if trying to decide which of them was more likely to give her what she wanted.

"No, I don't think so," Jimmy said.

"Our part's finished, though," Steve said. "Excuse us."

He started to move past her, but she cut off his escape by stepping between him and the door. "Wait! Can't you tell me how it's going?"

Jimmy looked at Steve and laughed. "Guess you'll have to hear it from someone else, Miss Harrison."

Audra took hold of Jimmy's lapel, and he looked up at her. "You never called me, Jim. You promised."

He smiled painfully. "Guess I must have been busy."

Her calculating stare made Steve cringe, and he decided that for once his friend needed some help. "Come on, Jimmy. Three more hours on our shift."

"Right." Jimmy eased away from Audra and shrugged a little, then turned his back to her and walked toward the door. Steve followed him out and down the granite steps.

"Thanks."

Steve smiled. "No problem."

"There's something about her, you know?"

"Yeah, something toxic."

"No, I mean it. She's very attractive."

"I don't see it."

"You're blind. I had to keep telling myself she hurt Lisa. Therefore she hurt you."

Steve looked at him curiously as he unlocked his pickup door. "So?"

"So, if I hadn't remembered that, I might have asked her to go out," Jimmy said with a sheepish laugh.

***

When Lisa left the courtroom, she was exhausted. She wanted to go home and go to bed, but she knew she had to go back to the office. They were far too busy for her to take the rest of the afternoon off.

She stepped into the hallway and looked toward the bench where Steve and Jimmy had sat. It was empty.

Her disappointment was sharp, and she realized she had counted on seeing them again. But at least she had a memory of Steve being decent and respectful and kind. For once, he hadn't annoyed her. And he had prayed for her. She knew he had kept the promise. Others were emerging from the courtroom, and she went to the coat rack and took her coat from the hanger.

"Excuse me."

"Yes?" She turned toward the woman who had spoken and caught her breath. She had only seen her once, but the image was burned into her memory. She must be a model, Lisa thought. If anything, her appearance was more sensational than when she'd seen her at the hospital back in February. She had a face that drew attention, and her clothing, makeup and hairstyle accentuated it. Funny, it struck her just then that this woman was exactly Bryan's type.

"You're Lisa Archer."

Lisa pulled her coat on and walked toward the door.

"Wait, please, Lisa!" The redhead was hurrying to keep up with her.

Lisa stopped and turned to face her. "What do you want?"

"Please, can you tell me how the hearing went?"

"You'd better ask Bryan." Lisa could see him leaving the courtroom, talking earnestly to his lawyer.

The red-haired woman turned to see, and Lisa headed for the doorway. She walked out into the cold, late November air and hurried to her car. She unlocked it with her remote and got in, not looking back. When she arrived at Clark Media, she parked and switched the engine off.

"I will not cry," she said aloud. She took a deep breath and looked in the mirror. Her face was white. She sat for another minute, slowly regaining her equilibrium.

When she stepped off the elevator upstairs in the office, Mindy jumped up eagerly from her desk.

"How'd it go?"

"Not bad. The judge listened to me, the cops, and Bernard Smith, then tossed out Bryan's lawsuit."

"Hooray!" Mindy came around her desk to hug her. "I prayed so hard!"

"Thank you. I appreciate that." Lisa turned toward her office, then paused. "I saw your brother."

"Really? Did you speak to him?" Mindy seemed to find the topic fascinating.

"Yes." Lisa's mind was still in turmoil over the events at the courthouse, and she wasn't sure yet what all of it meant.

"So?" Mindy prompted.

"He's not so bad. I shouldn't have let him upset me before."

Mindy smiled. "He's a pain sometimes, but he's really a great guy, Lisa."

Lisa considered that, and nodded. "Well, anyway, that's over."

She went into her office and stood at the window. Was it over, or was it starting again? The lawsuit was gone, but Steve Rollins was back in her mind and her heart. For nine months she had worked to keep him out.

It was disconcerting to admit it, but seeing Steve had unnerved her more than coming face to face with Bryan again after so long. At least she hadn't needed to speak to him directly. Bryan was the same as ever—every hair was in place, and his tie was the perfect complement to his tailored shirt and elegant suit. In contrast to Steve, ruggedly handsome in his uniform and just a little disheveled from having paced the courthouse hallway for an hour, Bryan had seemed a bit dandified and insipid.

And the confrontation with the overdone redhead had unsettled her. Lisa was amazed that Bryan's clandestine girlfriend had had the nerve to approach her. They must still be seeing each other, despite what Bryan's mother had said, or she wouldn't have come to the courthouse. Lisa wondered if she shouldn't have been just a tad more civil.

No, she decided. Civility probably was not in that woman's vocabulary.

She went to her desk and sat down, opening the folder on Fossett's Seafood. The family's treasured photographs were beautiful, and the campaign was developing nicely. The gold bracelet was safely back in Mrs. Fossett's jewelry box, where Lisa would never see it again.

When she thought about it, she knew that things were going well all around. Why let the day's events rattle her? She had a good life, even though things hadn't turned out the way she'd planned. Her sister was expecting a baby. Mindy would have her own office in the art department in January. Bryan was out of her life forever. And Steve Rollins had been kind to her.

Feeling suddenly free, she went back to the window and flung it open. The tall maple was bare now, and the breeze ruffled her hair. The chill air swept into the room, and she breathed it in deeply. Then she laughed.

***

"Lisa was so odd when she came back from the courthouse," Mindy said to Steve that evening. "She seemed really tense at first. I guess it was hard on her, seeing Bryan again."

He tried to visualize Lisa when she saw Bryan in the courtroom. He would bank on her keeping her composure. But still, he wished he'd been able to walk in there with her, as a friend. To be there for her when the questions were tough. To be someone who would smile at her, even when the lawyers made her feel sad and angry. To be someone she could look at when she didn't want to look at Bryan. But did she really want that? Her behavior at the courthouse confused him. If she didn't find him repulsive after all, then what did she feel?

"I saw her today," he said quietly.

"She told me. She said you're not so bad."

His stomach lurched. It was a tiny thing, but still. "She said that?"

"Mm-hm."

"Did she seem happy that things went the way they did?"

"Yes, and relieved."

"Do you think …?"

"What?" Mindy asked.

"Never mind." No, he wasn't ready to call her again. He'd tried that once, and she had ignored him. He realized now that he'd been more hurt by that than he would have been if she'd called and said she didn't want to see him. If she spurned him again, he knew it was forever. He couldn't take that chance. Instead, he would hold on to the slim possibility that they might meet again one day, and she wouldn't look on him with revulsion.

The memory that stayed with him was her asking the bailiff if he could go with her. Over and over, he replayed it mentally. She'd wanted his company. Jimmy's, too, of course. That took the edge off it. It wasn't *him* she'd wanted. It was moral support. Once again, she'd wanted someone to be there for her when she was having a crisis. That was all he was good for, it seemed.

Maybe he should just forget it. How many times could he rescue Lisa? He'd be foolish to wait around for another chance.

CHAPTER THIRTEEN

Steve stood staring at the tiny card, trying to decide what to write. Two weeks had crawled by since he had seen Lisa at the courthouse. He couldn't stand it any longer. If she didn't want to see him, fine, but he had to know.

He'd finally come to the conclusion that he had to take the risk. He'd gotten as far as a florist's shop and chosen his peace offering, but now he couldn't decide what to put on the card.

He wrote her address firmly on the envelope: Lisa Archer, Clark Media, 207 Maple Avenue. That part was easy. But the message. A few words could mean so much. He had to get it right.

Lisa, it was great to see you again. No, that wasn't strong enough. *Lisa, so glad things went well in court.* If he'd sent it the next day, that might make sense, but he'd waited two weeks, and they were into December. *Merry Christmas, Lisa!* No, too generic, and it didn't seem to match the flowers.

Lisa, I'd love to see you again. Maybe that would do it. It would leave her an opening. If she chose not to follow up on it, he would know there was no hope. He wrote the message on the card and scrawled his name as the florist put the flowers in a box and gave him back his credit card.

His cell phone rang. He pulled it from his pocket and looked at the incoming number. The fire station.

"Rollins, we need you. Are you done with lunch?"

"Yeah, I'll be right there." He hung up and turned to the woman behind the counter. "I've got to run. You'll deliver those this afternoon?"

"Within the hour," she assured him.

****

"Lisa, there's a delivery for you."

Lisa groaned. She didn't have time for this.

"Okay, but I can't come out there."

"No problem," Mindy said.

Lisa tried to go on with her drawing, but her concentration had been broken when Mindy buzzed her extension. She was pushing herself to get ready for an important presentation on Friday, and everything was going wrong. The copier was broken, the door to the library was jammed, and she had spilled coffee on her skirt that morning. Now she had another interruption to deal with.

A few seconds later, Mindy knocked perfunctorily and opened Lisa's door. "Right in here." A uniformed delivery girl carrying a large box followed her into the room.

"What on earth?" Lisa stood up.

The girl set the box on her desk.

"Lisa Archer?"

"Yes."

The girl smiled. "Sign here."

When she was gone, Mindy lingered. Lisa supposed it was a bit of an event for her, a little mysterious, and the most exciting thing that had happened in the office since the bracelet had been delivered.

"Hurry up," Mindy said with a chuckle. "I can smell them, and it's driving me wild."

Lisa reached out and lifted the cover of the box hesitantly. She gasped as she saw two dozen perfect pink roses and greenery nestled in dark green tissue paper.

"Oh, lovely," Mindy breathed. "Who's it from?"

Lisa's heart tripped as she pulled the small envelope from among the stems. It was a lavish gift, and she couldn't imagine who would be so extravagant for her sake.

"That's funny. There's no card."

"None?" Mindy's eyes were wide.

Lisa sat down heavily. Her stomach knotted with anxiety. "I don't understand."

"Looks like you've got a secret admirer."

"No, it's some mistake," Lisa said. Men didn't send her roses. Well, Bryan had a couple of times, but not to the office.

"Maybe it's the new creative director, Todd Blanchard. He's been making excuses to consult you all week."

"Oh, no, it can't be from anyone in the office. Can it?" Lisa was appalled at the thought. It would be unprofessional for one of the executives to send her flowers at work. A sudden thought came to her. "I hope they're not from Rod Greer."

"Oh, I'll bet they are," Mindy said, her face clearing. "He's crazy about you."

"No, I told him off before the hearing. He hasn't come around me since."

"So, maybe he's trying to start something again."

"Oh, please." Lisa sat back in her chair, eyeing the box warily. "I'm not sure I want them. I mean, if he doesn't have the nerve to sign his name—"

"Maybe it's a really sweet, but shy fellow," Mindy persisted. Her eyes lit up. "Marty Griffin, in the mailroom."

"Wonderful," Lisa said sarcastically. No, it had to be someone with money, someone who wanted to impress her, but in a showy way.

"How about Rick?"

"He quit calling me months ago. There just wasn't any chemistry there."

"So, maybe he's trying to start a reaction."

Lisa laughed mirthlessly. "I don't think so."

Mindy snapped her fingers. "How about Mr. Clark?"

"The company president? That's ridiculous."

"No, really, think about it. You've done great work all year, and he knows you've got this huge client presentation Friday, and you're probably nervous. So he sends you flowers to perk you up."

Lisa shook her head. "It doesn't feel right. He never does anything like that. An upbeat memo, maybe, but not this. Besides, he would have signed it."

"Oh, well, I think you ought to display them prominently, just in case," Mindy said.

Lisa put out a finger and stroked one of the soft petals. "If they're from some moron like Rod Greer, he'll get the wrong idea."

"But if they're not …"

"All right," Lisa sighed. "Can you find a vase? I've really got to get back to work."

"Sure. Oh, and the locksmith will be here in the morning to fix that lock on the library, but the copier guy can't come 'til Monday."

"Great," Lisa said grimly.

Mindy took the box away, and Lisa pulled a storyboard toward her. Too bad they weren't from Steve Rollins. But no, Steve was direct. He wouldn't play games like that. If he wanted to get to know a woman, he'd make it clear. He'd seemed concerned about her at the courthouse, and a glimmer of hope had risen in her heart. But it had been two weeks, and the only thing he had made clear by his absence was that he wasn't interested.

***

"Lisa got flowers today at work."

Mindy was cooking supper for two, while Steve sat at the kitchen table paying bills.

"She did?" He looked up from the checkbook.

"Yeah, it was really weird."

"How weird?" His pulse started hammering. Had she thrown them in the dumpster?

"There wasn't any card."

Steve felt a kick in the pit of his stomach.

"No card?" he said weakly.

"Right. An anonymous admirer. Really gorgeous roses, though."

He stood up quickly, shoving back his chair. He ought to call the florist, but it was after hours. He looked at Mindy. She was calmly stirring a skillet of beef and vegetables.

"What did she say?"

"She wondered who sent them. We tried to figure it out."

"Did she reach any conclusions?"

"Not really. I made her keep them in case one of the bosses sent them. She was a little afraid they were from Rod Greer, I think."

"Who's he?"

"The wolfish company lawyer."

Steve swallowed.

"Or they could have been from Rick," Mindy said, reaching into the cupboard for two plates. "Lisa says not. She gave him the gate last summer, but if he liked her a lot, I think he might take another stab at it."

Steve reached in his pocket where he kept his cell phone. His hand closed around it and a small piece of cardboard.

With dread, he pulled it out and looked at it. *Lisa, I'd love to see you again, Steve.* A tiny bouquet was printed on it, and the florist's logo.

He sighed.

"What is it?" Mindy asked. She stopped halfway to the table with the plates in her hands.

Steve tossed the card on top of the electric bill and walked into the living room. Maybe this relationship was doomed from the start. Maybe the two of them just weren't meant to be together. He could accept that, if he just knew. And if he could get rid of the feelings that swept over him every time he thought about her.

He opened the drapes and stared out into the darkness. Across the yard, there were lights in the house on the next street. Some people over there had normal families. The men came home at night and kissed their wives and played with their kids. They knew they were loved, that their families were solid and permanent. He wanted that, but it seemed less and less likely each day that his craving would ever be satisfied. He had to forget Lisa and find someone else to think about. If he didn't, he'd go crazy, and he'd grow old alone.

"Steve."

Mindy was right behind him. He took a deep breath. Her hand was soft on his shoulder.

"Steve, what happened?"

"My phone rang while I was fixing the card, and I got distracted. I didn't realize it until just now."

"You've got to call her," Mindy said with conviction.

"No, I can't call her."

"Of course you can."

"No." He felt like he was going to be sick.

"Come on, you're not a nervous person. Just call her and laugh it off. *I had an emergency, and I forgot to stick the card in the envelope.* She'll understand. It would be a relief to her, to know who sent them."

"I doubt it."

"Oh, Steve."

He turned to face her. "She still hates me."

"She does not."

"Oh, yeah? Well, she sure doesn't like me."

"How do you know?"

"You said yourself, she thought of half a dozen guys who might send her flowers, and I wasn't one of them."

"She didn't mention you," Mindy admitted.

"You didn't think of me, either."

"Well, I did, but only for a second. I didn't tell her, because I figured if it was you, you'd have sent a card, or marched in there to deliver them yourself. You've never hesitated to say what you think."

Steve swallowed hard. "It seems like every time I tell Lisa what I think, she ends up furious. I can't call her."

Mindy gazed at him mournfully. "Let me call her."

"No!"

She winced.

"Sorry." Steve turned away.

"She wasn't mad when you saw her at the courthouse, was she?"

"No, but she was under a lot of stress that day."

"How serious is this for you?"

He looked off out the window.

"Those roses were really something," Mindy said softly.

He took a deep breath. "I haven't been able to look at another girl since February."

"I knew there were sparks between you, but every time you got near each other it seemed like a three-alarm conflagration was imminent."

"Something like that." The coals were still smoldering in his heart, but it seemed he would have to bank them again, and put the old longing to rest.

Mindy shook her head. "I thought you deserved it when she was angry with you, but it seemed like you couldn't stand her, either. You should have told me."

He looked at her sharply. She was very close to Lisa now. He didn't like feeling that he couldn't trust her with his most private thoughts. "Just, please, Mindy, don't say anything. You can't tell her any of this."

Mindy hesitated. "All right, if you really want to go on like this. Come on, let's eat. And don't tell me you're not hungry. I've worked all day, and I want someone to appreciate my cooking."

Steve put his arm around her and headed for the kitchen. "All right, sis. Tomorrow night, supper's on me."

"Oh, I have a date tomorrow."

Steve stopped and stared at her accusingly. "It's your birthday. You can't do that. I'm taking you to a fancy restaurant."

"I'm sorry. You didn't tell me, so I told Mark I'd go out."

"Mark? I thought he was away at school."

"He just got out for Christmas break."

Steve ran his hand through his hair. "Well, how about lunch, then?"

Mindy smiled. "Lunch would be perfect. Pick me up at the office."

"Oh, no you don't. I see what you're trying to do."

"What?" Her brown eyes were wide and innocent.

"You want me to come to Clark Media to get you, so I'll see Lisa again."

Mindy scowled. "It was a thought."

"Yeah, well, just keep your thoughts to yourself. Where do you want to eat lunch?"

"I can pick?"

"Of course."

"How about the Red Jacket? I've always wanted to eat there, but it's wickedly expensive."

"Be there at noon."

***

Lisa was frantic Thursday morning. The presentation for Coastal Real Estate was not coming together the way she had imagined it would, and one of the artists was out with flu. She had less than twenty-four hours to work a miracle.

Mindy came and leaned on the doorjamb, watching her search through files and loose papers for an elusive sketch.

"Can I help?"

"Not unless you can convince the clients that they want to put this off until after Christmas."

"I don't have that kind of clout," Mindy said.

Lisa nodded. "I don't, either, or, believe me, I'd be on the phone. Oh, where is it?"

"What?" Mindy asked.

"This." Lisa straightened with a sheet of paper in her hand, relief flooding over her.

"Steve's taking me to lunch," Mindy said.

"That's nice." Lisa sat down and pulled a file toward her. She had to make this work, she had to. Mr. Clark had spoken to her that morning of his expectations for the project. The roses had been relegated to the top of her file cabinet in case the boss had sent them, and their fragrance filled the office, but she didn't really believe Mr. Clark was the giver. Now Mindy was in the mood to talk about her brother, but Lisa couldn't take time to listen. She would not let anything sidetrack her today. Not even Steve Rollins.

"Come with me?" Mindy wheedled.

"You're insane."

Mindy looked hurt. "Because of Steve?"

"No, because I'll be shot at dawn if this presentation isn't ready." She scribbled notes furiously, but she was having a hard time keeping her train of thought. She could feel Mindy's eyes on her. She wrote on for several seconds, then stopped and threw down the pen.

"Okay, you're right." She met Mindy's baleful stare. "It's because of Steve. Are you happy?"

"No. Actually, I'm very unhappy about you and Steve. You're making each other miserable."

"That's ridiculous! Do you really think I'd allow a man I hardly know to make me miserable?" Lisa tried to laugh, but an inexplicable sorrow surged up from deep inside her, and she crumpled into tears. She hid her face in her hands and tried to hold back a sob.

"Lisa, I'm so sorry. Forgive me. I shouldn't have bothered you now, when you're so busy." Mindy was beside her, a hesitant hand on her arm.

Lisa stood and held out her arms, and Mindy hugged her.

"Listen to me, okay?" Lisa choked.

Mindy nodded.

"I can only say it once. Your brother means nothing to me. Because I mean nothing to him. This thing is all in your head, Mindy. You're a very gifted, imaginative person, and you're imagining something that isn't there. I saw him two weeks ago, and he was very nice that day, but he hasn't made any effort to contact me since then, so he obviously doesn't care."

Mindy opened her mouth, then closed it.

"Look, I really need to finish this project," Lisa went on. "We'll talk later, okay? I don't want lunch, I want an uninterrupted hour to work. And even if I were hungry, I wouldn't go out with you and—" she shrugged helplessly. "I just wouldn't."

***

Mindy followed the hostess to the table where Steve was waiting for her. He stood when he saw her and held her chair. She looked like a savvy career girl, but unspoiled. His sister. He was proud of the way she was turning out.

"Hi!" She landed a kiss on his cheek before she sat down. "You wore a tie. I'm impressed."

"Happy birthday." He held out a gaily wrapped package.

"Thanks." She opened it eagerly, discovering a leather-covered diary and a silver pen. "Thank you! This is so luxurious. I'll have to write important thoughts in here."

"Your thoughts are always meaningful." He was feeling gallant and brotherly.

Mindy smiled and folded the wrapping paper. "This is really cool," she whispered, glancing around the elegant dining room.

"Well, take a good look, because it will probably be a while before I bring you here again." Steve picked up his water glass.

"Did you know this is the marriage proposal capital of Maine?"

"I saw the commercial."

"Bryan used to bring Lisa here all the time."

"Did you have to?" He put the glass down.

"What?"

He sighed. "Did you have to bring up Lisa, first thing?"

"She's my best friend."

"So? I don't come in here and immediately start telling you all the clever things Jimmy said this morning."

"Sorry. I asked her to come with us, but she was right out straight today on a big campaign."

The waitress placed their food in front of them, and Steve watched in silence. *As if Lisa would have come to lunch with them.*

After he asked the blessing, Mindy picked up her fork.

"You didn't tell her, did you?" Steve asked.

"No. You made me promise."

"Good. Don't breathe a word."

"But you wanted her to know in the first place. You *did* write a card to go with the flowers."

"That was before I knew how far she'd banished me into mental oblivion."

Mindy said nothing, but began to eat.

Steve cut into his steak. He *would* stop thinking about her. It was the only solution.

"So, did you open the box Mom sent you?" he asked.

"No, I thought I'd open it when I get home tonight. I'm hoping it's a new jacket. That's what I told her I needed."

Steve glanced toward the doorway and stopped chewing. "I don't believe it."

"What?" Mindy looked over her shoulder, then back at him. "What?"

"Dr. Charming."

"Bryan Cooper?" Mindy looked again. "That's him?"

"Sure is. I never saw the girl before. Quit staring."

Mindy jerked her head around toward him. "But she cries out to be stared at!"

Steve shook his head in disgust. "She can't be over eighteen."

Mindy took another glance, surreptitiously this time. "That's what I call a micro-mini skirt."

Steve tried to keep his eyes on his plate, but Mindy sneaked another look.

"Whoa! That dress really needs a back. She must be freezing."

"I told you not to stare, infant."

"Oh, relax. It's obvious she likes attention." She studied Steve's face as she resumed eating. "You look tired. Are you working tonight?"

"I get off at six."

"Good. Go to bed early."

"I'll think about it." He felt sometimes that Mindy was taking care of him, although she was four years his junior. "If you're out late, though, I'll be worried about you."

"You don't have to worry when I'm with Mark."

"You really like him, don't you?" Steve had met Mark a few times, and he seemed level-headed and steady, though not very exciting.

"He's very nice, but I'm not jumping into anything. I want to be sure before I commit."

"Things have cooled off with Jimmy, then?"

She chuckled. "Things were never hot with Jimmy. He's a riot. Period."

Steve nodded. Movement across the room caught his eye. "Well, looks like you're not the only birthday girl."

Mindy whirled around. "Maybe she's nineteen today."

Steve shook his head. "Someone ought to warn her."

Mindy turned wide eyes on him. "Stephen! That looks like a jewelry box!"

He looked again. "Incredible. Don't turn around again." Bryan Cooper had looked in their direction. Steve put his napkin to his mouth.

"What's he doing?" Mindy hissed.

"Watching her open her 18-karat gold charm bracelet."

"You're pulling my leg."

"Nope." He couldn't make himself look away as the girl leaned animatedly toward Bryan, her eyes glowing.

"I've got to see it!" Mindy whipped around and stared.

"Mindy, good grief! Turn around!"

"After everything he put Lisa through, you'd think he'd have learned something."

Steve shrugged. "It's safer than a ring, I guess, for a man who's not after commitment. Oh, she's holding it up. Looks like there's only one charm on it. I can't tell for sure."

"Well, that's how you start out," Mindy said. "You don't get them all at once. You collect them over time." She took a bite of her chicken cordon bleu.

"Audra Harrison had a ring," Steve said thoughtfully.

"You said it wasn't a diamond."

"No." His eyes strayed back to Cooper's table as he ate. "Now he's putting the bracelet on her wrist."

"I'm going to get a better look." Mindy stood up abruptly.

"Hey, no, wait—!"

It was too late. Mindy was striding across the dining room, toward the restroom on the other side. She wove between tables so that she passed by Cooper's.

"Oh, what a beautiful bracelet!" It was so shrill, Steve could hear every syllable. He put his hand to his forehead in despair.

"Oh, thank you," the girl said, eyeing Mindy uncertainly.

"Do you mind? I'd just like to—oh, how cute! A German shepherd. You know, my friend, Lisa, had one just like it."

Steve thought Cooper's eyes would pop out.

"Really?" the girl said faintly.

"Yes, she had a lot of charms. Tennis racquet, sailboat, oh, and a little Christmas tree. Her boyfriend gave her the bracelet. It was really sweet. A cupid for Valentine's Day. She never got a ring, though!" Mindy smiled at Bryan and the girl. Bryan looked decidedly ill. "Well, thanks. Have a good lunch!" She swung on toward the ladies' room.

Steve got up and went quickly to the checkout and paid for their meal. He stood in the foyer, and when Mindy left the restroom he signaled to her.

"What, no dessert?" she pouted.

"I'll buy you an ice cream cone," Steve said. "Come on."

"I had to score one for Lisa."

"You are something else."

CHAPTER FOURTEEN

At five o'clock, Mindy began tidying her desk. Co-workers passed her, heading for the elevator. She opened her top desk drawer and took out the little florist's card. It was so tiny, but it meant so much. She glanced down the hallway toward Lisa's office.

She started to get up, then sat down again. If she didn't actually *tell* Lisa, just let her see the card…She could make it seem accidental.

No, that would be a betrayal of Steve's trust.

The company president came down the hallway, swinging his briefcase.

"Good night, Mr. Clark."

"Good night." He pushed the button for the elevator, then turned toward her. "You did say the locksmith will be here tomorrow for sure?"

"First thing in the morning."

"Good. Al Decker almost locked himself in the library this afternoon."

The elevator opened, and Mr. Clark got in Mindy waved as the door closed. She picked up the florist's card and sighed.

She loved Steve a great deal. He'd always been assured and self-reliant, never timid, but where Lisa was concerned, he seemed to have lost all his confidence. She didn't think she liked that in Steve. If she could just tell Lisa…But she had promised.

She loved Lisa, too. Lisa was the sister Mindy had always longed for. It wasn't right for the two people she cared the most about to be so uncomfortable with each other. The lengths Lisa and Steve went to in order to avoid each other were becoming ridiculous, and Mindy was having to carefully arrange her schedule so that the time she spent with each of them would never overlap. It was silly.

Rachel West came down the carpeted hallway carrying a soft tan briefcase. "'Night, Mindy."

Mindy smiled and waved, then sat irresolute for a moment. It was nearly half past five, and the office was almost deserted. She stuffed the card in her pocket, walked to Lisa's door, and knocked.

***

Lisa looked up briefly, then back at her desk. "Hi."

"Looks like you're getting there," Mindy said.

"Yeah, but the copier's still broken. I had to take the whole thing out this afternoon and have it copied and collated, but at least I'll have something to hand the clients in the morning."

"You should have told me. I could have done that for you."

"No, you were too busy with all those prospective clients coming in."

"Mm. They seemed to like the creative staff. Maybe we'll have another big account to work on after the holidays." Mindy hesitated. "Are you going home?"

"Not yet. There's one more thing I need to check on. Demographics stats. Something just didn't look right, and I need to be sure."

"Can I help?"

"I don't think so, thanks." Lisa rubbed her eyes.

"Better quit for tonight."

"Soon."

Lisa knew she meant well, but their fondness for each other was becoming an emotional drain. Since the hearing, every time she talked with Mindy, she started thinking about Steve, and she didn't have the time or the courage for that.

Mindy hovered for another moment in the doorway, then went away. Lisa pored over a government report, but the data she needed just wasn't in it. She got up and headed for the door, taking a sheaf of papers with her. When she passed the reception area, Mindy was putting on her jacket.

"Good night."

Mindy smiled mournfully and gave her a little wave.

Lisa went into the windowless library, flipping on the lights, and pulled out a drawer of the periodical file. Somewhere in here was the snippet of information she needed.

Behind her, she heard the door close. It took her a second to realize what had happened. Walking quickly across the room, she grabbed the doorknob and tried to turn it. When it refused to function, she rattled it.

"Mindy? Hello! Is anyone out there?"

Mindy's voice came faintly, then closer. "Oh, Lisa! Are you in there? The lock—oh, man! The locksmith won't be here until tomorrow!"

"Call him!"

"All right, I'll try. Just hang on, Lisa. I'll go see if I can get hold of him."

Lisa took a deep breath. She wasn't claustrophobic, and Mindy would get help. She might as well finish the job. She located the report she needed and sat down at a desk to make notes.

"Lisa?"

"Yes?" she called toward the closed door.

"Someone's coming to get you out."

"Thank you."

"Did you find what you were looking for?"

"Yes, I'm reading the file now."

"I really shouldn't have shut the door."

Lisa thought Mindy sounded distressed. "It's not like you tried to lock me in here," she said with a smile.

Mindy said nothing.

"Can you get me the file folder on my desk and shove it under the door? I think it will fit. The one that says *Henderson*?"

"All right." Two minutes later, the folder slid beneath the door. Lisa went over to retrieve it.

"Mindy?"

"Yeah?"

"Thanks."

"You're welcome."

"Hey, don't you have a dinner date? You don't have to stay."

"It's okay," Mindy said. "I think everyone else has left. I'll at least wait until the guy gets here."

"Thanks. Where are you going?"

"I'm not sure. Mark's surprising me."

Lisa gasped. "It's your birthday. I forgot your birthday."

"It's all right."

"No, it's not. That's why your brother took you to lunch, isn't it? I got so busy! I'm sorry, Mindy."

"Forget it."

"No, I will not. And as soon as this lock is fixed, I'll give you your gift. It's been in my desk for a week."

"Really?" Mindy sounded genuinely touched.

"Yes. I'm not always this scatterbrained."

"You're just stressed," Mindy said stoutly.

It was a comfort to know someone sympathetic was just beyond the door. She and Mindy got along so well, they could share most of their worries and problems. There was really only that one thing they couldn't talk about.

"I'm glad you're here," Lisa said. Suddenly she felt she couldn't go on indefinitely without resolving the issue. It wasn't fair to Mindy, and she didn't want to go on for years with a forbidden topic she could never discuss with her best friend. "Mindy, are you there?"

"Yes. I won't leave you."

"Thanks. I don't want anything to come between us."

"Besides the door, you mean?"

Lisa chuckled. "Right. I was thinking more of…you know. The one thing we can't talk about. Or maybe I should say, the one person."

"Steve."

"Right."

"Let's not let that ruin our friendship," Mindy agreed.

"You're my best friend," Lisa said, leaning against the door. "I don't ever want us to fight or get angry because of Steve."

"All right." Mindy sounded tearful. "Let's promise that, no matter what happens with Steve, we'll still be friends."

"I promise," said Lisa.

"Me, too."

Lisa took a deep breath and slid down to sit on the floor. "You keep saying he cares about me, but I don't see it."

"I know he does."

Lisa sighed. He had a funny way of showing it. He had sat by her in the hospital, but anyone might do that. He'd seemed concerned at the apartment while she was ill. She was fuzzy on what she had said that day, but it seemed a turning point, when his dislike had deepened. His disdain for her in her senseless allegiance to Bryan for three years seemed to have peaked that day. Maybe it was because she had refused to see Bryan's family. Did he think she was heartless? Her heart had been in shreds.

That day in the supermarket, when he'd dropped the eggs, he'd looked so surprised and wounded, she'd wanted to laugh. But then he'd have come back at her with some snide comment, deliberately embarrassing her again. Or would he?

Then she hadn't seen him for so long, the hurt had almost healed. But running into him at the courthouse had ripped the wound open again. She'd had a glimpse of what they could have had together, if they'd started out right. She truly believed he had a tender, loving side. But it wasn't for her. He had only derision for her. How long would it take the hurt to heal this time?

From beyond the door, Mindy called, "Lisa, the elevator just opened. I'll be right back."

Lisa waited for the locksmith with tears streaming down her cheeks. She had thought she saw a pattern in Steve's actions: doing what was needed in a crisis, taunting her, then disappearing. His gentleness at the courthouse didn't seem to fit that pattern. Was it remorse because of the past? Or did he really, truly care? The tears came faster.

She heard a man's voice, then Mindy's, and scrambled to her feet and across the room to fetch her papers.

"Right down here. This door."

"Lisa?"

She faced the door in shock. It couldn't be.

"Lisa, can you hear me?"

"Y-yes." It was.

"We'll have you out in a minute. Are you okay?"

"I'm fine."

Mindy was supposed to call the locksmith, not her brother. Lisa looked at the watch pendant she wore around her neck. She had stopped wearing a wrist watch, or anything around her wrist, after the accident. It was just past six o'clock. Probably the locksmith was closed, and Mindy had called the one person she knew she could count on.

Slowly, Lisa walked to the door. She could hear them talking on the other side. She slid down and sat again, leaning against the wall. Just hearing his voice made her pulse quicken.

"Can you open it?" Mindy asked.

"Yes, but it will take a couple of minutes. I'll have to dismantle the lock set."

"That's okay, as long as you can get her out."

"Oh, I'll get her out." He sounded grim. Lisa could imagine the firm set to his mouth. He didn't sound happy to be there.

"Look, I should go," Mindy said nervously. "Mark and I—"

"I think you'd better stay," Steve said.

There was a thump, then the scrape of metal on metal.

"Don't look so glum," Steve said. Lisa could hear him so plainly it hurt.

"I feel so guilty," Mindy said.

"What for? Your stunt in the restaurant?"

"No, not that."

"You didn't tell her, did you?" He kept his voice low, but Lisa picked it up.

"About Bryan in the restaurant?" Mindy asked. "No."

Lisa turned her head so that her ear was at the crack between the door and the jamb. She wanted to say, *You saw Bryan today?* but she held it back. She didn't really want to know what Bryan was up to now.

Steve said, "You didn't tell her about the other thing? You promised."

Mindy was silent.

"Melinda Ruth! You promised." It was louder, and Lisa jumped a little. Her pulse raced. He was angry, or worried, about something he didn't want her to know.

"I didn't tell her."

She heard his sigh, even through the door, and wished she could see his face. Straining her ears, she heard him say, very quietly, "When this door opens, I will be on the elevator. You got me?"

Lisa felt fresh tears in her eyes. He couldn't even stand to look at her now. Her lip trembled. She looked around frantically. On a cabinet on the far side of the room was a box of tissues. She got up silently and went to get it.

When she returned, wiping at the tears, she heard Mindy whisper fiercely, "I told you, she doesn't hate you! If you just tell her you sent the flowers, she'll understand. Steve, listen to me! She's an intelligent woman. She—will—understand!"

Lisa felt as if the wind had been knocked out of her. The flowers. Steve had sent the gorgeous roses. What did it mean? She stared at the door, hearing the scraping sounds he made as he worked on the lock in merciless silence. She felt sorry for Mindy.

Dear Lord, I've had enough of this, she prayed silently. *Please help us put it to rest.*

She took a step closer to the door and touched the pine panel with her fingertips. He was just beyond it. She could feel the wood vibrate as he worked.

She took a deep breath and said clearly, "Steve, you sent me the flowers?"

There was an absolute silence.

Mindy hissed, "I didn't tell her. I swear I didn't tell her!"

"Lisa?" His voice was low, tentative.

"Yes." It came out in a little gasp.

Another long pause. Then, very soft, "I sent them."

Her lip trembled. She swallowed hard. "Thank you. They're beautiful. I'm—glad to know who it was."

"I meant to send a card with it," he said mournfully.

Mindy piped up, "Lisa, he really did. He got an emergency call, and he forgot to put it in the envelope. He wouldn't have sent it anonymously on purpose."

No, Lisa thought, *he wouldn't. If a swashbuckler like him was going to send flowers, he'd sign his name with a flourish.*

"I've got it right here," Mindy went on. "Lisa, look at this."

"Hey—" Steve began, but he broke off.

A small piece of paper came under the door. Lisa picked it up off the rug and looked at it. It was a florist's card, with a picture of a bouquet and the scrawled words, *Lisa, I'd love to see you again, Steve.* She held it gingerly, unable to quite connect those words with the suspicious bouquet in her office. But it had to be true. Steve had written those words, and he had meant them. Her hope rekindled, leaping up inside her.

"Okay, Lisa, you're a free woman."

The door swung open. Lisa's breath caught as she stood face to face with him. Neither of them seemed able to speak. She looked deep into his eyes, warily expecting to find disgust or disdain there, but all she saw was anxiety.

CHAPTER FIFTEEN

Steve couldn't say a word. He just stood there stupidly, holding the screwdriver.

Lisa spoke first. "Thank you, Steve. Seems you had to rescue me a third time. The escalator, the accident, and now this."

"The third time's a charm," Mindy said brightly.

Steve scowled at her.

"Oops. Sorry. I said the forbidden word." Mindy hung her head in remorse.

Lisa frowned, then gave a short laugh. She stepped out into the hallway, and Steve turned back to the door and made the final adjustments that brought the entire lock assembly loose. He tossed the screwdriver in the toolbox and closed it.

"I'll leave all the parts here for the locksmith to mess with tomorrow," he said to Mindy, picking up his toolbox.

To his surprise, Mindy burst into tears.

"Are you all right?" Lisa asked, stepping toward her.

"No." Mindy looked very young and miserable. Lisa held out her arms, and Mindy buried her face on Lisa's shoulder. Steve stood watching in confusion. As far as he could see, Mindy had no reason to cry.

"Will you forgive me?" she sobbed. "I'm so sorry."

"For what, honey?" Lisa asked gently.

"I just wanted to help. If you want to be mad at me, okay, I deserve it, but please don't be mad at Steve anymore."

"I'm not mad."

Mindy sniffed. "Steve told me not to tell you about the flowers, but I couldn't stand for you two to be hurting each other, so I locked you in there on purpose. Please forgive me."

"Don't cry. It's all right." Lisa held her close, looking at Steve over Mindy's shoulder.

Steve shook his head in disbelief. "You deliberately locked Lisa in? Are you demented?"

"No. I love you both very much, and I couldn't stand seeing you suffer any longer. I just wanted you to see each other and talk. I'm sorry. If you can't forgive me, I'll understand." Mindy's eyes were red and bleary. She pulled away from Lisa and walked dejectedly down the hall toward the reception area.

Steve looked at Lisa. There were tears on her cheeks, too, and her green eyes were troubled. He took a deep breath. "Lisa, I'm sorry, too. For everything I said and did that upset you, from the first day we met."

"It's all right," she said softly. "Some people just never get along."

He felt a deep, mortal pain when she said that. She was killing his hope, if she thought they could never be friends.

"I know you don't want me here, so I'll go now." His voice caught.

"Wait. I couldn't help hearing through the door." She didn't meet his eyes, but he stood still to hear what she would say. "I never hated you, Steve."

"You didn't?"

She shook her head.

"You kept telling me to leave you alone."

She spoke slowly, earnestly. "When I realized Bryan wasn't everything I'd thought he was, you were the last person I wanted around to see me deal with that." She looked up at him with a grimace. "You knew too much."

"Lisa." He wasn't sure what to say. He wanted to take away all the hurt and disappointment she had endured, but he knew that wasn't possible.

Her lips turned up just a little, in a tiny smile. "You looked at me that day on the escalator, and I felt like you saw right to the bottom of my heart. How I'd trusted Bryan all that time, and how foolish I'd been. You sized him up pretty accurately the first time you saw him, but it took me years!" She shook her head.

Slowly, he put the toolbox down on the rug. "You were so unhappy then. It was pretty obvious that things weren't going well. All I ever wanted to do was to make you happy again, but it seemed like the only way I could do that was to get out of your life. It's what you wanted."

"No, it's not what she wanted!"

They both whirled to face Mindy. She had come back, softly down the hallway, carrying a box of tissues.

"Don't you two understand anything? Lisa, you needed time to recuperate and grieve, but then you needed some comfort. You were just too stubborn to let people who cared about you comfort you. And you, Steve. Your stupid pride wouldn't let you tell her how you felt, because you were afraid of being hurt. If you love someone, you ought to be willing to take that risk."

Steve realized he was staring at her, his mouth open. He closed it and threw a sidelong glance at Lisa. She was staring at Mindy, too.

"I'm leaving," Mindy said. "I am sorry I locked you in, Lisa. But I'm not sorry you're together, if only for a few minutes. I suggest you go get something to eat and talk things over."

She put the box of tissues in Lisa's hand and walked away.

Lisa took one and wiped her eyes carefully.

Steve leaned back against the doorjamb. "You're beautiful, even when you're crying."

Her face wrinkled, and for a moment he thought she would snap at him.

"You're still here," she said, but this time she was smiling. Tears clung to her lashes.

"Do you want me gone?"

"No. Never again."

Steve swallowed and looked down at his boots. It hurt a little bit to breathe.

"I never meant to hurt you," he whispered.

She stooped and placed the tissues on top of the toolbox, then straightened, putting one hand out, not quite touching his sleeve. "I think it was mostly my fault."

He shook his head adamantly. "No, I was an idiot, and I was rude to you."

"I was worse. I told you to leave when you were trying to help me."

"You were sedated. I thought you really meant it, though."

"So did I. But I didn't. Oh, Steve, I didn't." She was crying in earnest.

He bent and pulled a tissue out for her, then stepped forward, wrapping his arms around her. She collapsed against him. They stood in the hallway together for a long time. Steve rubbed his cheek gently against her hair.

"Lisa, I've loved you so long. I tried and tried to think of how I could get you to forgive me, but it seemed like two people who grated on each other's nerves like that probably didn't belong together. And that made me very sad."

"I'm sorry I did that to you."

"I was stupid. I know I made you mad."

She nodded miserably. "You did. I was mad because you could see what I hadn't seen. And I was mad at you for coming into my life at the wrong time. But the thing that made me absolutely furious was that I said go, and you went. Steve, don't go away again. Please."

His arms tightened around her. "You mean it?" His voice was ragged as he held her, with her head firmly against his shoulder.

"Yes. Do you think we can work out the rest?"

He smiled. "Absolutely."

She pushed away from him a little and looked up at him. "I had to stop comparing you to Bryan. Every time I did that, it made me hate myself. I wasted so much time and energy on him. And then I drove you away. I've tried to forget about you all these months, but I couldn't stop thinking about you."

He bent to kiss her, and Lisa melted against him, her right hand covering the badge on his chest, her left creeping slowly up around his neck. She ran her fingers gently through his hair as he kissed her.

"I love you," she whispered, and he crushed her to his heart.

It was enough. He decided Mindy was right, and he would risk it all. "Lisa, will you marry me?"

She was very still for a moment, then she stirred.

"You mean that?"

"Yes."

"It's so sudden."

"No, it's not. Not for me. I haven't been able to think about anyone else since that day on the escalator." He kissed her ear, then her temple, then the corner of her eye. "I love you. I'm miserable without you. Be my wife."

"Yes."

He leaned back against the library doorframe and pulled her with him, relief and joy flooding over him. "Lisa, listen. I want to go to a jewelry store tonight. We can get dinner somewhere after, but first I want to buy you a ring." He lifted her hand to his lips.

She hesitated.

"Please," he said. "It's important to me that we get it tonight. I told myself once that if I knew you loved me…well, I don't want to wait another hour before I give it to you."

She was crying again.

"I'm sorry." She dabbed ineffectually at the tears. "I'm a mess. I'd better go home, don't you think?"

"No. You're beautiful. Please don't go home. If you want to change or something, okay, I'll wait. But I want you to be wearing my ring tonight."

Still she wavered.

He bent down and looked at her closely. "You did say you'd marry me."

"I meant it."

"Good. Then what is it? Tell me."

"I don't want anything fancy."

"No, just a regular diamond ring."

"Not too big," she whispered.

"All right. You pick it out."

"A plain band."

"Yes. And plain gold wedding bands to match. We'll get them tonight, too. I don't want a long engagement."

"You know I'm a little more cynical now than I used to be."

"It's okay. I wouldn't want you to just accept me without a good, hard look."

"You can forget about Bryan?" she asked.

"Who?"

She laughed, and her eyes held a sparkle that he'd yearned to see. "All right, let's go."

***

When they left the jewelry store, Lisa was supremely happy. The street was resplendent with Christmas lights, and it was snowing lightly. She kept lifting her left hand and peering at the diamond by the glow of the streetlights. It was cold, but she kept her gloves in her pockets. Her right hand was nestled in Steve's warm one, and she didn't want to cover the ring on her left.

He put his arm snugly around her as they walked across the large parking lot. The snow crunched under their boots, and falling crystals sparkled all around them. Lisa breathed in the cold, crisp air. Nothing could take away the joy she felt in that moment.

They reached his truck, and he took out his keys. Lisa smiled up at him, and he bent to kiss her gently. She couldn't resist putting her hand up to fluff the snowflakes from his hair.

"I love you," he whispered.

If I'm any happier, I'll explode, she thought.

"Lisa?"

She turned toward the voice. Bryan stood staring at them. He looked very prosperous and proper in a wool overcoat and a fur Cossack hat.

"Bryan!" She felt Steve stiffen beside her.

"Yes. I thought that was you."

Lisa smiled. "Bryan, may I introduce my fiancé, Steve Rollins?"

Bryan stepped closer and looked sharply at Steve. "I believe we've met."

"Could be," Steve said. His eyes were cold. "I'm at the hospital a lot."

There was a pause.

"You're well?" Lisa asked.

"Yes. My ankle still bothers me sometimes, but …" His eyes roved from Lisa to Steve and back. "You're getting married?"

"Yes, we certainly are." Lisa laughed as she said it, unable to contain her happiness.

"When?" Bryan sounded bleak.

She hesitated. They hadn't set a date yet, but Steve had said he didn't want a long engagement.

Steve spoke up firmly. "Christmas Eve."

Lisa schooled her face to keep from showing surprise.

Bryan's eyebrows went up. "So soon?"

"Yes," Lisa said decisively. "Just a small, family wedding."

"Well, congratulations." Bryan turned and walked toward his car. Lisa noted that it was an older model sedan, not at all like the showy new sports car he'd bought the year before.

She turned to face Steve. "You're quick."

"Too precipitous?" A smile played about his mouth.

"Not a bit. Christmas Eve is perfect. The ultimate Christmas gift."

"Really?" He brushed her forehead with his lips. "Because I was thinking maybe you'd rather have jewelry," he said with an easy flippancy that delighted her now that it was no longer mingled with sarcasm.

"Oh, no. I've sworn off jewelry. Except this." Lisa held her left hand where she could see the sparkle of the diamond.

Steve pulled her into his arms.

"Who was that guy, anyway?"

THE END

For your enjoyment, here are the first scenes of Susan's romance novel *She Gets July*, Book 1 in her new Mainely Romance series.

Rebecca froze when she spotted a postcard nestled innocuously between the phone bill and an L.L. Bean catalog. An eagerness she would have denied made her fingers shake as she picked it out of the day's handful of mail, and she read it with bittersweet satisfaction. Rob was faithful, even though she had released him from all commitment three years ago.

Dear Rebecca, I've checked things out and turned on the water and electricity. Any time you want to use the cottage, it's ready for you. RW

She stared at the neat, backward-slanted printing he had developed in grammar school, and tears came to her eyes. She dropped the postcard to the table and went to her bedroom to change out of her nursing uniform, determined to put Rob Wallace out of her mind.

She fixed herself a sketchy supper and carried it to the living room, where she ate it while watching the local news. When she took her dishes to the sink, she realized she was avoiding the table because she didn't want to see the postcard again, and she didn't want to think about Rob.

But the cottage was still an important part of her life, even if Rob wasn't. She picked up the card and flipped it over to examine the address side. It was the plain manila card sold in the post office, not the scenic kind, with lovely Maine vistas enticing you to get away for the weekend in Vacationland.

That was just what she would do. The cottage was hers for the rest of May, and she would go up this weekend. The ice had barely gone out of the lake, and the water would still be too cold for swimming, but she could sit on the dock in the late spring sun and have a fire in the stone fireplace in the chilly evenings. And she could get out and walk for miles on the dirt roads near the lake, satisfying her latent longings for the country.

Of course, there would be reminders of Rob everywhere. She didn't need any photos to see him, even after all this time. In her mind's eye, he was there, bent over the postcard with the pen in his left hand, frowning in concentration over the address, his brown eyes placid and his chestnut hair fluffy and tousled.

Her eyes stung, and she blinked hard. It was worth the painful memories, to get away from Portland for a couple of days and blow the cobwebs from her brain.

She wavered, looking down again at the words he had written—when? Yesterday? The day before? The postmark said May 4. Saturday, two days ago.

She hadn't seen him in more than three years. They'd talked on the phone a couple of times, briefly. It was business only, to tie up loose ends concerning the cottage. He never tried to see her when she drove an hour to the north to use it. But the postcards had come every spring. *Rebecca, the cottage is ready.*

Rob sat at his computer, fine-tuning an elevation for a new elementary school. In a few more hours, he'd be done with the project, but he didn't really want to be finished. Between projects, his mind drifted too much, and he didn't want that right now.

He'd been out to the cottage Saturday, to check on things and make sure it was ready for Rebecca. It was May, and she'd be going there soon. May was hers, then he would move to the lake for a month.

On the last day of June, he would pack up all his things and move from the lakeside, back to his parents' home, so she could claim the cottage for the month of July. And on the first day of August, he would move back to the lake. It happened every year. People thought it was strange. Fine, let them think that.

His phone rang, and he picked it up.

"Hi, honey. Ready for lunch?"

Rob winced, but he was too polite to tell Brittany how uncomfortable her syrupy greeting made him. "Uh, sure. I'll meet you downstairs in a couple of minutes." He saved the computer file and stood.

"The princess beckons?" Eric, at the next desk, was a good friend, but he enjoyed needling Rob. "The chains of slavery are tightening."

Rob scowled at him. "What do you suppose your wife would say if she heard you talking like that?"

Eric grinned. "Leah would say, 'That's right. Eric's been my slave for seven years.' And she'd be right."

"You've only been married five." Rob reached for his jacket.

"Trust me, friend, it starts long before the wedding. Look at you, scrambling every day at noon."

"Twice a week," Rob said. "I told her I can't do lunch more than that."

"Oh, so you're in control, not Brittany. I'll bet you're Johnny-on-the-spot Friday nights, too. Next thing you know, she'll have you picking her up for work every day, even though it's miles out of your way. You might as well marry her now."

That hit home. Brittany had suggested he pick her up in the morning, but Rob had begged off. He shrugged. "Hey, it's not that serious."

Eric nodded doubtfully. "Right. You've been dating how long?"

"Just a couple of months."

"Mm-hmm. Two months."

"Or three. I forget."

"Tell me she hasn't been hinting for a diamond."

Rob frowned. "It's pretty early for that, don't you think?"

"So? Talk isn't enough for a woman like Brittany. If you don't cough up a tangible token of your adoration—preferably a ring—pretty soon, she'll make you miserable."

"Did Leah do that to you?"

"Well, no, but Leah's nothing like Brittany. Not her type at all."

Rob headed for the elevator shaking his head. He wasn't ready to make things exclusive with Brittany, let alone permanent, but he wasn't about to admit it when Eric was implying that marriage was a deathtrap. Eric made no secret of his opinion that Brittany was the wrong choice for Rob, and he couldn't resist ribbing him every chance he got.

Maybe Eric was right. Brittany was a bit of a clinging vine. She definitely wanted to move things along faster than Rob did. If Eric wasn't so cynical, maybe Rob could talk to him seriously about the relationship. But he knew what Eric would say. *Run, do not walk.*

You can find *She Gets July* at Amazon.com, in both paperback and eBook editions.

About the author

Susan Page Davis is the author of more than one hundred published novels. She's a two-time winner of the Inspirational Readers' Choice Award and the Will Rogers Medallion, and also a winner of the Carol Award and a finalist in the WILLA Literary Awards. A Maine native, she now lives in Kentucky. Visit her website at: https://susanpagedavis.com, where you can see all her books, sign up for her occasional newsletter, and read fun features on her "Freebies" tab. If you liked this book, please consider writing a review and posting it on Amazon, Goodreads, or the venue of your choice.

Find Susan at:
Website: https://susanpagedavis.com
Amazon: https://www.amazon.com/Susan-Page-Davis/e/B001IR1CGA
BookBub: https://www.bookbub.com/authors/susan-page-davis
Twitter: @SusanPageDavis
Facebook: https://www.facebook.com/susanpagedavisauthor

More of Susan's Novels you might enjoy

Contemporary Romances:

She Gets July
Off the Record (releases August 2022)
Trail To Justice
Alaska Weddings series
   Always Ready
   Fire & Ice
   Polar Opposites
Love Comes to the Castle
Revolution at Barncastle Inn
Short and Sweet (short story collection)

Mystery and Romantic Suspense:

True Blue Mysteries:
   Blue Plate Special
   Ice Cold Blue
   Persian Blue Puzzle
Skirmish Cove Mysteries
   Cliffhanger
   The Plot Thickens (releases November 2022)
The Maine Justice series:
   The Priority Unit
   Fort Point
   Found Art
   Heartbreaker Hero
   The House Next Door
   The Labor Day Challenge
   Ransom of the Heart
The Saboteur
The Frasier Island Series:
   Frasier Island

    Finding Marie
    Inside Story
Just Cause
You Shouldn't Have
On a Killer's Trail
Hearts in the Crosshairs
What a Picture's Worth
The Mainely Mysteries Series (coauthored by Susan's daughter, Megan Elaine Davis):
    Homicide at Blue Heron Lake
    Treasure at Blue Heron Lake
    Impostors at Blue Heron Lake
Tearoom Mysteries (from Guideposts, books written by several authors):
    Tearoom for Two
    Trouble Brewing
    Steeped in Secrets
    Beneath the Surface
    Tea and Promises
    Tea Leaves and Legacies

Historical novels:

Homeward Trails Series:
    The Rancher's Legacy
    The Corporal's Codebook
    The Sister's Search
The Outlaw Takes a Bride (western)
Counterfeit Captive
Almost Arizona
River Rest (set in 1918)
The Crimson Cipher (set in 1915)
Mrs. Mayberry Meets Her Match
Hearts of Oak Series (Co-authored with Susan's son James S. Davis, set in the 1850s):
    The Seafaring Women of the Vera B.

The Scottish Lass
The Ladies' Shooting Club Series (westerns):
    The Sheriff's Surrender
    The Gunsmith's Gallantry
    The Blacksmith's Bravery
Captive Trail (western)
Cowgirl Trail (western)
Hearts in Pursuit (western novella)
Christmas Next Door
Echo Canyon
The Prairie Dreams series (set in the 1850s):
    The Lady's Maid
    Lady Anne's Quest
    A Lady in the Making
Maine Brides series (set in 1720, 1820, and 1895):
    The Prisoner's Wife
    The Castaway's Bride
    The Lumberjack's Lady
Seven Brides for Seven Texans
Seven Brides for Seven Texas Rangers
White Mountain Brides series (set in the 1690's in New Hampshire)
Wyoming Brides series (set in 1850s):
    Protecting Amy
    The Oregon Escort
    Wyoming Hoofbeats
The Island Bride (set in the 1850s)

And many more! **See all of her books** at https://susanpagedavis.com.
Sign up for Susan's occasional newsletter at https://madmimi.com/signups/118177/join